DEMETER'S TABLET

THE NIA RIVERS ADVENTURES BOOK 2

INES JOHNSON

THOSE JOHNSON GIRLS

Manufactured in the United States of America
First Edition July 2017
Second Edition October 2020

There was a difference between growing up and growing old. Growing old was the process of aging. It was the accumulation of changes in body and mind over time. The body wrinkled and turned gray. The mind expanded with knowledge, only to learn years later that its sage collection was now obsolete in the new day.

I understood why humans didn't want to succumb to Father Time and instead changed their bodies with cosmetic and medical procedures. Why people resisted the drag of years by surrounding themselves with items and ideologies of their youth, holding on to a past that no longer had a place in the present.

Growing old was a cruel fact of life. But growing

up—the taking of responsibility for one's actions; the standing at attention to face an uncertain future; the acceptance that, in the grand scheme of things, one person was insignificant and would be forgotten in a matter of time? Yeah, that was a buzzkill that deserved to be ignored for as long as humanly possible.

Unfortunately for me, I wasn't human.

I tried to sink my ancient bones down into the depths of the waters, but my youthful flesh was too buoyant, too resilient, and I floated back to the top. As an Immortal, my body didn't age. I would never grow old. It was my mind that creaked and ached under the weight of time. I shoved the nagging pressure of my responsibilities for the past, present, and future aside and came to the surface.

I floated in the baths of Budapest, my body weightless in the mineral waters. The Budapest thermal baths were said to rejuvenate the body and help preserve age, not that I needed it.

On the deck, a few women lay out in the moonlight. Their stomachs were flat and their asses were high. When they smiled, their faces barely moved. Their breasts defied gravity. It was their wrinkled hands that gave them away, telling the true tale of their age. My eyes were sharp enough to see the gray roots peeking from their expensive dye jobs.

In the waters, an old man in a Speedo delivered his best lines to a svelte coed, who was a quarter of his age by the looks of her. She turned to her friends, and they pointed and giggled at his outdated attempts. Undaunted, the man floated to another side, bypassing all the age-appropriate women basking in the moonlight, to find the next sorority girl.

I swam into the middle of the coeds. Even though I was older than their minds could comprehend, they took one look at my physical body and accepted me into their group. I waved my toned arms in the air and gyrated my trim body alongside the crush of sweaty, young bodies singing about never getting older and being a rebel youth. As if any of them knew anything about age and rebellion.

Out of the corner of my eye, I caught my friend, Loren, motioning to me. She mouthed the words, "Come here," urging me to get out and join her. I turned my back on her, not ready to return to work, to the reason we were here in Budapest, to my responsibilities. I wanted a night of being stupid and immature. So I rebelled and pretended I was young.

I shoveled tumblers of alcohol down my throat

and brushed against mostly naked bodies in the waters. I was surprised when Loren didn't pull me bodily from the waters. Normally, she had the attention span of a gnat, but she could be single-minded when she was on a mission. Instead of tugging me out, she only shrugged and gave me a look that told me I'd regret it. I didn't doubt it. The cheap alcohol burned a hole in my throat even as my immortal cells worked double time to repair the damage.

"Excuse me? Are you German?"

I turned to a lanky young man dressed in board shorts. His chin had yet to grow into his facial hair. I shook my head in response to his query.

"Oh, that's too bad, because I want to be Ger-Man. Get it? *Your man.*"

"Really? Is that the best you got?" I stared at the guy, waiting to see if he could produce some other come-on. When I didn't tug on his line, he retracted his rod from my little area in the waters and cast his net wider.

I floated away, scoping out the masculine bodies as I glided through. My body caught many gazes, but none that I cared to hold. I hadn't dated in over five hundred years. Over the last dozen decades, I'd gone to balls, fairs, and clubs that were filled with eager men, ripe for the picking for any woman who could bat an eyelash and crook a finger. I didn't understand why modern women had trouble getting dates. There were dozens of unattached males at every turn. Many were in these waters.

I immediately caught the eye of another young man. This time, our gazes held as he made his way over to me. His eyes were a light brown hooded with dark, lush lashes. I couldn't immediately pinpoint his heritage from his facial features. He could have been Mediterranean or Middle Eastern. He had a defined chest with a smattering of hair that happily trailed down. The rest of him was tall with sun-kissed skin.

"Can I get you another drink?" he asked.

I nodded.

When he returned, he said, "I'm Aydin."

"I'm Nia. Aydin is a Turkish name. Is that where you're from?"

"My father is from Turkey; my mother is from Hungary."

I let out a chuckle. It came out a little forcefully since it had been several weeks since I'd laughed. "I'm sure dinners at your house must be interesting with that kind of heritage."

Aydin cocked his head, his thick eyebrows squished with incomprehension.

"You know," I prompted, "because the Ottomans conquered Hungary five hundred years ago."

His face remained an array of puzzled pieces.

"Based on that, I assumed there might be fighting at the dinner table between your parents?"

He cocked his head to the side, but the movement did not bring the pieces of the historical picture together. "They did?"

I wasn't sure if his words were a question or a statement. Had I just opened an old wound about his dysfunctional family? Or did he truly not know his own history? He had to know the Ottoman Empire had invaded this land. Their influence was everywhere—from the smell of paprika that spiced the evening air to the very baths we were pruning in.

"Wait..." Aydin gave a shake of his head. "Who were the Ottomans again?"

I opened my mouth but then closed it. A full moment passed as I stared at the kid. In the end, I decided to swallow my judgment. In older times, people didn't get much of an education outside their trade. Perhaps the school systems in Budapest weren't that good? There were plenty of other things to talk about besides history.

"So, are you on holiday, Nia?"

"Business trip," I said. "I'm taking the night off. Enjoying the baths." I couldn't help myself. Another history lesson burst forth. "Did you know it was the Ottomans who introduced the practice of bathing to the Magyars?"

"The who?"

The Magyars were the people who lived on these lands before the Germans. What were they teaching the youth in these schools? I threw up my hands, both literally and figuratively.

"You know, Aydin, I think I'd better check on my friend."

"Wait, Nia. Do you mind if we go Dutch on this drink?"

I blinked, almost launching into a lecture about how 'going Dutch' was actually a derogatory phrase. It hailed from the seventeenth century, when England and the Netherlands fought over political boundaries and trade routes. But instead, I decided to go find the Dutch woman I had come with.

"You know what, Aydin? It's fine. I'll take care of it."

"Sweet." He grinned. "Are you on the 'gram?"

"The what?"

"Instagram. So we can talk."

"You want to talk with me on a computer app used for pictures?"

"Yeah." He nodded and bent over his phone in its waterproof casing.

"You wouldn't want my phone number?"

"What for?" he asked, cradling his phone in his palm, caressing it with his thumb. He no longer made eye contact with me.

"Right," I said. "Look me up under CroftyGirl."

"How do you spell that?"

"Ask Siri?"

I headed for the steps that would take me out of these troubled waters. But I didn't make it home free.

"Excuse me," said a dimple-cheeked frat boy with an American accent. "But your breasts are like Mount Rushmore. My face should be in the middle of them."

"OMG, I am too old for this shit."

Another moment in these waters surrounded by juveniles of any age would drive me into early retirement. I turned and climbed out in search of Loren. Once out of the healing waters, the weight of the unwanted memories left me feeling old and weary. I wanted to sit down next to the cougars lined up in lounge chairs and shrivel up.

"Had enough?" Loren asked when I joined her.

"How the hell can you stand dating in the twenty-first century?"

"I don't date," she said. "Like a modern woman, I use men only for what they're good for. Then I do everything else myself."

"And where has that gotten you?"

She turned her blonde head and glared at me with those baby blues. "Oh yeah, and dating the same guy for five hundred years got you what?"

I jerked at the low blow.

Loren grimaced, her hand coming to rest on my shoulder. "Too soon?"

I had broken up with my lover, Zane, over a month ago. Supposedly, time healed all wounds. In fact, there was some non-scientific study done in a women's magazine that said it should take half the time people were together in a relationship to get over their ex. In that case, I'd be mourning my relationship for the next 250 years.

Time didn't heal anything. As someone who'd been around for a very long time, I knew that all more time did was allow people to make new wounds. If this was all the dating world had to offer me, I might join a convent.

"I have good news," Loren said. "I think I found our man."

My eyes lit up. But then I realized she didn't mean Zane. We were after her ex-lover, a guy who had an in with a cult that promised everlasting life. I'd remembered hearing about a tablet depicting the sacred rites of such a group—the Ninnion Tablet. But it had gone missing a while back.

We'd been chasing after Loren's ex since we'd left France a few weeks ago. Normally, I worked for the IAC, the International Antiquities Coalition. But I didn't feel like going on a dig in a remote part of the world. I didn't feel like being surrounded by a group of crusty old men who would second-guess things I knew to be true because I'd lived them.

None of my old colleagues would listen to me bitch about their gender. None of them would understand the need to redo my pedicure two days after I'd gotten it done. Not even one would comprehend the validity of retail therapy. No, what I needed was some good old-fashioned girl time, sprinkled with a little adventure, with a healthy side dish of male bashing on the side.

"I just got a tip that Leonidas Baros is out on the town tonight," Loren said. A wide grin spread over her face, and her blue eyes twinkled at the mention of her ex's name.

My gaze narrowed. "You seem awfully eager to see him."

Perhaps she heard the irritation in my voice, because she quickly rearranged her features into nonchalance. "Well, yeah. So we can solve this case. We're gonna uncover history, shine the light on marginalized cultures, 'cause that's what we do. And if we happen to get lucky along the way, well, then everybody wins."

"I thought we were taking a break from exes. What did you say?" I asked. "'Hoes before bros.'"

"I'm not trying to get back with Lenny. I don't do repeats. Well, except that one time I saw him in Prague. And then we did bump into each other in Rome a couple of years ago. But other than that, no repeats."

I arched an eyebrow at her.

"But," she continued, "I do think you need to get a little something-something while we're on this trip, just to take the edge off your breakup. Maybe *a lot* of the edge off. You can toy with these little boys if you want." She waved her fingers at the boys playing at men in the water. "But I think you might need a man. Lenny always has a nice group of men around him. You can take a bite out of one of them while I . . ."

I cocked my head and pursed my lips at her.

"While I get the information we need, of course."

"Whatever, let's go check this lead out."

"Not so fast." Loren blocked me with her arm. "We may be a little overdressed."

I looked down at our bikinis. Then I crossed my arms over my chest. "Loren, what have you gotten us into now?"

CHAPTER TWO

We left the hedonism of the baths and headed for holy ground. Mátyás-templom, or Matthias Church, sat atop a hill aptly named Buda Castle Hill. Its turrets stretched up into the darkened night. On the roof, colorful tiles gleamed in the moonlight. The architecture was a marriage between Ottoman mosque, Jesuit temple, and Roman Catholic church.

"Here, put this on." Loren handed me a lace mask.

I was still in a bikini and heeled sandals from the baths. We'd slipped on shear cover-ups before we'd hopped in the car. The mask would cover more of my face than the swimsuit covered my body.

"Why do I need a mask?" I eyed it suspiciously. It

reminded me of a party I'd gone to in Paris thrown by the Marquis de Sade.

"It's kind of a costume party."

Loren and I had only known each other for two months. But a lot had gone down in that time—life and death situations, breakups, makeups, a little mass genocide. We'd seen each other at our best and our worst. We'd had a chance to learn each other's habits and quirks well. So when she didn't meet my eye, I knew something was up.

"Loren?" I elongated the two syllables of her name.

She turned around, exasperated. "All right, it's a sex party."

"Loren!" I stomped my foot against the car's floorboard, eyeing the door handle.

"We're just going to go in, find Baros, question him, and get out."

"Loren . . ." I sighed, turning away to look out the window at the cityscape passing us by.

"It's either this or we go to a museum and try to decipher the writings of the Eleusinian Mysteries on pottery."

I grimaced. I loved museums, but she knew I hated riddles. Even more, I didn't want to sit in my room moping, or worse, go back to the baths and be hit on by Millennials. I needed something to do. If this guy, Baros, was a quick route to finding out more about the mysterious cult, I supposed I could risk my virtue for one night.

"Are you sure you're not trying to get back with this guy?" I asked.

"No." She didn't meet my eye. "Baros and I are over. I'm here for work, not play. Besides, you're still in that mourning period where all guys are jerks. Since I'm your best friend, I won't break the girl code."

Loren had taken the title of *my best friend* shortly after we'd met. I hadn't bestowed it upon her—she'd just claimed it. Like I was a newfound land and she'd staked her flagpole in my chest. I didn't mind. It was nice having someone watch my back.

"But a sex party," I whined. I wasn't a prude. I'd been to orgies before. I was alive during the heyday of Rome. Had been present and accounted for during the writing of the *Kama Sutra*. And for those romance readers who got a kick out of the new wave of BDSM books? Yeah, they should have lived through the Victorian age.

Although I didn't have a youth, I did my fair share of sexual rebelling. But that was all before I'd met . . . him. He who should not be named while I was trying to get my groove back. I fidgeted with the mask on my face. The lace itched my cheek.

"You don't have to do anything," Loren said. "And if anybody makes a pass at you, you can just break their mortal fingers. Everything will be fine. This is the best lead we've got to learn about the Eleusinian Mysteries."

While they'd been together, Loren's ex-lover, Leonidas Baros, had implied he knew the mysteries of the ancient cult. The rumors of the cult went back for hundreds of years. It invited all into its ranks, including rich and poor, male and female, philosophers and slaves. But the rituals the initiates undertook to get into the cult had never been revealed. All any outsiders knew was that, once accepted, the initiates were promised everlasting life, riches, and knowledge.

Immortals were the only beings on this earth gifted with a natural long life. There were others who were given or took immortality through supernatural means. Just recently, I'd learned that the natural privilege could be stolen.

An ancient tribe had killed two of my kind and drank an elixir concocted from their bones. The concoction had served to prolong the humans' lives.

The adults of that cult had been slain, but their children remained alive. For now.

My gut clenched at the thought that it could be happening again, had happened again. If there was something I could do to stop it now, then what was a little grope and poke along the way?

Loren and I got out of the car. We came to stand in line behind a slow-moving group of ... creatively-clad bodies. Instead of their Sunday best, these people were wearing the barest frills on top of their birthday suits. One scantily-clad young woman caught my eye.

"But I was told to come," she said. Her hands waved animatedly. "I'm with College Buzz, the website. I'm here to give the party a rating and review for my blog. Hundreds of coeds visit my site daily."

The doorman shook his head, his gaze impassive and impenetrable behind dark shades.

"But I was given an invitation." She held up a cream-colored paper with gold-embossed lettering. There was a depiction of a feather surrounded by wheat on the piece of paper.

Something pulled at the corners of my mind—had I seen that symbol before and it meant something to me?

The doorman barely gave it a glance. "There were no invitations sent out."

The young woman stood and glared at him for a few more minutes. "Lamest party ever. I'm totally going to Yelp about this." Then she turned and stormed away, crumpling the invitation and letting it slide to the ground.

"Next," shouted the doorman.

Loren stepped up and whispered something to him. He gave her a once-over and then stepped aside. Loren tugged my hand, and we slipped past the velvet ropes into the church.

"What did you say to him?" I asked.

"Lenny always has a password."

"What's the password?"

She turned to me with a grave look. "If I told you, I'd have to kill you."

I quirked an eyebrow, and she laughed. But she didn't give over the secret code. I turned my attention to our surroundings.

I'd been inside this church many times over the years. By over the years, I meant centuries. I'd visited when it was first built. Watched as they built the high tower and hung the bell. I'd been in the chapel when the people hid the Madonna and child statue from the invading Ottomans. And now, hundreds of years after the Turks had fled the city and the mosque had become a church again, mother and son stood unveiled inside the chapel to see all the sin that had been let into the doors in the night.

This Leonidas Baros must indeed be rich, or at least well connected, if his pockets were deep enough to turn a holy church into a den of sin. People sat with bare asses in the pews and milled about with strong drinks. Some made out near the walls with murals depicting the Crusaders defeating the Turks. On the raised platform was where the real action went down.

A golden-haired man lay in a pile of women. Most of the women were nude or nearly there. The blond Adonis was decked out in his birthday glory while the women gyrated around him. One woman captured his lush lips. It looked as though he devoured her with his kisses. When she came up for air, another took her place, and he gulped her down, too. On and on it went. He never seemed to tire, yet the women appeared to lose their breath and needed a break from his embraces. Still, they kept going back for more.

He chuckled as one woman's eyes fluttered closed after a kiss and she appeared to pass out. He looked up in search of another. That was when his gaze caught mine.

I watched his nostrils flare as he surveyed me from head to toe. His gaze was proprietary. He traced the outline of my curves like he'd taken the route before. When his gaze found mine again, his eyes twinkled. No, the irises sparked like a lit match. Or a crack of thunder.

He crooked a finger in my direction, beckoning me closer. His lips moved, forming words I couldn't hear. But then a voice resonated inside my head. Was it his? I felt hypnotized. My feet took a step toward him without my permission. I halted my body and backed away.

He threw his head back and chuckled. A woman took that opportunity to catch his lips, drinking deeply from him. I had the urge to march over there for a taste of my own. But I didn't.

His lips stayed locked on the woman kissing him, but his thunderous gaze found mine again. He winked at me while his mouth worked her over. Somehow, that gesture communicated that it wasn't over between us. That it was, in fact, the middle. But there had been no beginning. Had there?

This man was just that—a man, a mortal. I knew every one of my kind. There were only ten of us left now. No one new had been born, or so we thought. I didn't remember my birth or my parents . . . if I even had any? There was one theory that Immortals sprang into being fully formed. But this man didn't give me a tingle or a twitch of the weakness that came when I was in the presence of one of my race.

He could be something else. There were witches and wizards in this world—mortals who could manipulate the energy of ley lines. There were also demons—mortals who gave up their souls to demigods. There were shifters; humans born with an animal soul. There were even honest-to-god knights—a group of men entrusted with safeguarding magical relics. Their exposure to that magic granted them certain powers and lengthened their lifelines. But I knew those men. I did my best to avoid them and keep them from my treasures, as they avoided me to keep their treasures from my admittedly grabby hands.

I couldn't tell those meta-humans from an ordinary one. At least not on sight. They had to reveal themselves to me. By looking at him, this guy didn't come off as wizard, demon, shifter, or knight.

Still, the prickles at my neck rose from intuition. There might be something magical about him. But I wouldn't find out now. I turned away from the libertine and found Loren moving steadily toward more velvet ropes.

She leaned in and whispered something to the man at the door. He looked her up and down and then removed the link. We were let through the ropes and led into an opulent room I hadn't seen in the church before.

A tall man with broad shoulders framed the picture window that looked onto the market below. Leonidas Baros looked like he'd walked out of an Olympic stadium. His cheeks were chiseled. His dark hair fell in a mass of curls around his face. His body was smooth, polished marble. All he needed was a sword and shield to be ready to take on any opponent who met him in the arena.

I could see the appeal. When I looked at Loren, it was obvious she was having second thoughts about her decision to end their relationship, or whatever had been between them. She appeared to want another helping of Baros.

"Lenny," Loren purred in what I was coming to know as her sex-kitten voice. She'd gotten us drinks at the bar last night with that tone, out of a speeding ticket while we were in the south of France, and into an upgrade on our flight to Hungary.

"Lolo."

The two embraced with a kiss on each cheek followed by a wet smack on the mouth that lingered longer than was friendly.

"It's been too long," Baros said, perusing her body. "The last time I saw you was at the end of a blade."

"That may have been because your own sword was sheathed in someone else's scabbard."

"Had I known you cared, you would've been given exclusive use of my entire arsenal of weapons." Baros's large hand glided down Loren's barely covered body.

"So maybe you should make me a permanent fixture?" Loren said.

She leaned in as Baros closed the last inch of distance between them. I cleared my throat to remind Baros that I was in the room and to remind Loren that we had another purpose here besides having her loins girded. Neither of them paid me any heed.

"Loren Van Alst, are you proposing to me?" Baros's lip quirked up.

Loren's face twisted in horror. "What? God, no."

Baros chuckled, completely undaunted at the rejection. He lifted his hand and ran his fingers through Loren's golden locks. A copper ring on

Baros's right hand caught my eye. It was a small ring, likely a woman's. It sat above the knuckle of his pinky finger. It was the Greek lettering that interested me.

His hand went over his heart, giving me another glance of the ring and allowing me to read the inscription. To many, it would look like chicken scratch. But to me, someone who could read every language ever written, the message was clear.

"Then to what do I owe this unexpected reunion?" Baros asked.

"You invited me to solve a mystery once," Loren said. "You said if I passed the tests, I'd be granted something beyond my wildest dreams."

"Did I say that?"

"You did," Loren said. "You said I was just the type of person they were looking for."

"Who's they?" I piped in.

They turned to me. Loren gave me a look that said, *Chill, I got this.*

Baros gave me a look that suggested he was contemplating whether I was friend or foe.

"Dr. Nia Rivers." I extended my hand.

Baros glanced at it suspiciously. Instead of offering his own, he crossed his hands over his massive chest with the ring facing outward. "Doctor of what?"

"Antiquities," I said. "I have a love of Greek history, like the ring you have on your finger. It looks to be from around 600 BCE."

"It's from 500 BCE." Baros grinned. "You have a good eye."

"It was stolen from Greece during the Nazi occupation of the Second World War, along with a host of other artifacts."

"Indeed it was. Although, they weren't the first scum to trample my homeland and take what wasn't theirs." Baros admired his hand. "I took it from the hand of a Nazi."

I got the feeling he meant that quite literally—that the Nazi's hand had come along with the ring.

"Many things were stolen from my people," Baros continued. "I have spent a lifetime recovering what was lost."

"You're an archaeologist?" I asked.

"No." He grinned.

"Ex-military?" I guessed.

"I never retired. War and conflict is a constant companion in this life. Once evil comes to rest, I suppose that is when I will, too."

His philosophy put a tick in his favor, but thieving was still thieving. "And now that you've recovered the ring, you'll return it to its rightful owner, I assume?"

"I have," Baros said.

"You're not the Greek government."

"Not anymore, no."

"That ring is over two thousand years old. It belongs in a museum." I felt the hackles on my back rising. That often happened before I found myself in a fight.

"Trust me," Baros said, making a fist with his ringed hand. "It's in the right hands."

Loren stepped between us, blocking my view of the large man and looking pointedly at me while she spoke to him. "Lenny, would you excuse us for just a second?"

She ushered me over to the side of the room, out of earshot.

"Correct me if I'm wrong," she said, "but you said you wanted to solve the mystery, not start a fight."

"That ring should be in a museum."

"*You should be in a museum.*" Loren took a breath and reached her palms out to me in a move I'd often done toward her when I needed to find patience. She took a deep breath and then tried again. "Do you want to see if this cult is legit or not? If not, it's cool. Because, trust me, I'd rather go skinny-dipping in the baths with Lenny over there."

We turned back to Leonidas Baros, whose back was turned. He leaned out the door, speaking to someone on the other side.

"Or better yet," Loren said, looking at his ass, "mattress-diving."

"We could just take it," I said, looking at his hand, which rested on the inside of the doorframe. The ring on his pinky gleamed at me, begging to be brought to a glass case in an air-controlled museum. "You said yourself these mortals can't stop me."

Loren looked at me with her eyebrows raised. "And I'm the one who's supposed to be the criminal?"

"Excuse me, ladies?" Baros shut the door and walked over to the desk. Reaching into a drawer, he pulled out two envelopes. "It is my great pleasure to inform you that you are invited to the Spring Eleusinian Mysteries."

I looked down at the envelope he presented. It was cream with gold-embossed letters, much like the one the young woman who was denied entrance had discarded. Only this one had the depiction of a lightning bolt within a crown of wheat decorating the top. Down on the desk was a stack of black and white papers with similar lettering and images. But that image, like the young woman's, had a feather. On the screen of the open laptop, a browser displayed the same feathered image on what looked like a message board.

Baros slammed the laptop closed and then placed the computer onto the stack of papers. His gaze narrowed on me, but I wouldn't be cowed for snooping. It was how I made my living.

"Why the change of heart?" I asked.

"Does it matter?" Loren said. "We're in."

"The initiation will take place a week from now on the spring solstice," Baros said. "If you are found worthy, all will be revealed to you. And Loren, I do hope you are found worthy."

Loren grinned at him. I felt like I was about to be in the middle of their private orgy. But Baros shook himself.

"I wish I had time to play, but duty calls." He motioned us toward the door with his right hand. "I hope you ladies will enjoy the rest of the church services."

"Wait." I planted my feet, motioning to the ancient artifact on his finger. "Name your price for the ring."

"It's not for sale." Baros's expression was harder than the metal of the ring.

"That's too bad, because I'm not leaving here without it."

Beside me, Loren groaned, and not in the good way.

CHAPTER THREE

I felt like Hercules facing off against all twelve labors in the form of one man. Baros was massive, broad and strong. He and I circled each other in the small space. The room was sparse. There were bookshelves on the far wall opposite the window. A desk took up space on the left of us, Loren on the right.

"Guys—" Loren began, but was cut off when I reached for Baros's right hand.

He blocked me with his left. Our hands did a windshield-wiping motion, making an arc. I cut through the arc, striking my hand in, and reached again for the ring. I got the tip of his index finger. I curled his finger inside my palm, but when I squeezed it back, his finger didn't bend. In fact, he smiled at my attempt to inflict pain.

That should not have happened. Not if he was human.

We were standing close to each other now, which gave me full view of his dark eyes. His completely dark eyes. The iris, the part of the eye that gave it color, was all black. There was no circled pupil in the middle. There was no white sclera, the outer part of the eyeball. His entire eye was completely dark.

Dammit. He was a demon.

I let go, and Baros and I sprang apart. We each took a fighting stance, me in a low crouch with my arms extended. He made himself even bigger, digging his heels into the floor and balling his fists. Into the middle of the fray rushed Loren.

"Loren, get back." Baros and I both shouted the warning at her.

Loren turned to face me. I assumed because she thought I could do the most harm. She likely thought I was going easy on him.

I wasn't.

I was stronger than a demon, but they could still put up a good fight. And Baros had already been born massive as a human, which worked to his favor. Add his natural strength with the unnatural power gifted to a demon, and that made him a formidable opponent.

Loren had been by my side through a battle of super humans before and had held her own. But if she got caught in the middle of this fight, she could get hurt. She was closer to Baros, and he grabbed for her, bringing her into his protective sphere, as though he was concerned for her well-being.

I cocked my head and stared. I'd never known a demon to care about anything other than itself and its master.

"Stay away from her, Lolo," Baros said, wrapping an arm around her waist and pressing her body into his. "You don't know what she is."

Loren knew exactly what I was, which was why I had to assume that, instead of lending me a hand and reaching for the cane in her shoulder bag to help me defeat this foe, she was making goo-goo eyes at the demon who held her within his clutches.

"Oh my God, Lenny," she cooed. "Are you trying to protect me? That's so sweet."

"That woman is dangerous," Baros said, shoving Loren behind his body. "I've met her kind before."

Once she was behind him and out of his immediate sight, Loren mouthed, "OMG," as though he had hung the moon with his ill-fated attempt at saving her life.

Hoes before bros, my ass.

"Loren," I said, "did you know your ex was a demon?"

Her eyes were wide and fixed on his broad shoulders. She looked at the fleshy blades on Baros's back like they were smeared with chocolate frosting. "I told you, I like the bad boys."

"No." I tried to reach for patience before reaching out and yanking the sense out of her. "I mean a soulless demon."

That got her attention. She pouted her lips, completely affronted. "Well, I wouldn't go that far."

"That's rich coming from a death-eating ghoul," Baros said.

"Excuse me?" I glared at him. "What did you just call me?"

"Hey . . ." Loren turned on him. "That's my friend you're talking about."

"Your friend is of a race of beings who have wreaked utter destruction all over the world for longer than time can remember," Baros said. "They have started wars and been behind mass genocides for millennia after millennia that continue to this day."

"Well . . ." Loren held up a finger, but it wobbled. "Maybe, but she didn't do it on purpose."

Loren turned to me for confirmation. I rolled my eyes and put my hands on my hips, completely letting go of my fighting stance in the face of this impasse.

"She's a Persian," Baros spat.

I raised my guard back up at the unexpected jibe. "No, I'm not."

At least, I didn't think I was. I spent a lot of time in ancient Persia, and the Ottoman Empire, and in modern-day Turkey. But I didn't think I was born there. I didn't have much of an affinity for the region. I didn't really have a loyalty to any part of the globe.

"Let me handle this," Loren said to me. She turned to Baros, placed her hands on his chest, and promptly got distracted. "Damn, Lenny, have you been working out?"

Baros broke his glare from me and grinned down at her.

"Oh, for the love of—" I blew out a breath, forgetting the Persia crack and putting my attention on my horny ho of a bestie. "Loren, look into his eyes. He has no pupils."

"He has a condition called aniridia," she said as

she gazed into his eyes. "He was born without pupils. It makes him sensitive to light. I think it's beautiful."

"It's the mark of a demon," I said. "It means he's sold his soul to the devil."

"I am a Chosen," Baros growled. "I didn't sell my soul to the devil. I gave it freely to my God."

"Who, I'm sure, is the devil," I said.

"You could say that," said a silky voice off in the distance. "In fact, most do."

I brought my gaze to the doorway. There stood the golden, kissable libertine in all his naked beauty. He was taller now that he was standing. As tall as Baros, but not as broad. He had a lithe beauty, like a gymnast with a muscle tone that looked like it was made for cuddling and not fighting. His abs looked like waves women would be eager to ride and let pull them down, down, down to a happy trail that led to a massive islet whose sail was raised as though eager to welcome me aboard.

I diverted my gaze. He was flanked by four men. A closer look at his bodyguards showed me they were without pupils and irises as well.

The libertine made his way over to me. Again, I felt drawn to him. He did have irises, but the color sparkled like golden flecks of lightning.

"Who are you?" I asked.

"I am crushed you don't remember me, Tisa."

I gulped, but my mouth was dry. *Tisa* wasn't an alias I used often. It was the first name I remembered, and only those who had known me for hundreds of years knew it.

"You said you had trouble with your memory from time to time." He chuckled again. "Get it? Time to time." He turned to the men behind him. They offered halfhearted chuckles at the attempt at a joke, but a moment too late. "I must admit, I am wounded you don't remember me after all we shared."

At his words, it was as though I shook a memory loose. I remembered his face grinning down at me, coming close to me from a time long ago. The sky was lit with every shade of yellow. Rain poured down around us, but not a drop touched our skin. In the present, I shook my head slowly, left to right. This could not be happening to me again.

Yes, *again*. I'd already forgotten a love affair with one Immortal. Somewhere among my things had to be a little black book where I kept these details of past affairs. Or maybe I didn't want to know who I'd shacked up with in the past?

"Oh, God." I cringed.

"Quite." Golden Boy grinned, taking another

step toward me. "Would you like me to refresh your memory?"

He reached for me. Those lush lips that had floored human women came at me. Instinctively, I stepped out of his reach.

He chuckled again. Then he turned to Baros and opened his hand. Baros's jaw clenched. The large male took a deep breath, nostrils flaring like a bull's. He reached with his left thumb and forefinger and pulled the ring off his right pinky. Baros clenched the object in his fist before he placed the ring in the libertine's hand.

"Is this what all the fuss is about?" Golden Boy asked, looking down at the ring.

"It belongs in a museum," I said.

"No," he said. "It belongs to me, and I gave it to Leonidas."

I paused. Who was this guy? *What* was this guy? Was he the devil who made these demons? He smiled as though he could see my thoughts. Was that a confirmation?

"Keep it for now," he said. "Return it when you remember. I'll see you in Greece? At the rites?"

My nostrils flared at the mention of the rites. I still wanted to know what they were. Golden Boy threw his head back and laughed, as though he knew he'd dangled catnip in front of my nose.

"Oh, Tisa," he purred. "My curious little Immortal could never resist a good mystery."

He smiled at me. His golden eyes raked over me from head to toe, leaving me feeling as though a lightning rod licked across my skin every place he lingered. His golden gaze met mine, and I saw the storm inside. I felt myself leaning forward, but before my lips touched his, I pulled back.

He sighed as though disappointed but not disheartened. It was a sigh that was full of patient mischief. "Let them go."

Golden Boy stepped aside and made a sweeping motion to the door. I didn't need to be told twice. I picked up my feet and headed in that direction. Then I turned, feeling as though I'd forgotten something.

"Loren," I hissed.

"Huh?" She turned from her continued appraisal of Baros. Looking crestfallen, she trudged after me like a kid who didn't want to leave the playground.

"See you soon, Lolo," Baros said.

Loren turned back with puppy-dog eyes. I yanked her out the door.

"You just had to have the ring," she grumped.

"It belongs in a—"

She pinched her fingers together and made a shushing sound. "Don't even. Especially when I know you're not about to drop that baby off at the Greek Ministry of Culture and Antiquities."

I looked down at the ring then back through the door at the golden man who was watching me walk away. I clutched the ring in my palm.

"Yeah," Loren said. "Thought so."

CHAPTER FOUR

My feet sank into the shaved earth. Granules sifted between my toes and settled on my toenails like a bronze nail polish. The pyramids stretched out before me. Tombs for kings, queens, and gods. The sun rose as I watched workers build the Temple of Isis.

They piled on sunbaked mud at the base. Stones of lime, sand, and granite fit together like puzzle pieces that reached higher and higher into the sky. The massive structure opened to sloping walls that showed high-ceilinged hallways.

I stood from somewhere on high, looking down at the progress. Arms encircled me, pressing the line of my body into the circumference of him.

"*Nefer baka, ashugee.*"

I wasn't entirely sure if this was a dream or a memory. I'd spent countless days and nights leaning back in the safety and comfort of his arms. There was nothing special about this moment, except the ancient language he'd used.

Languages were easy for me to remember, especially the original ones. The deep, familiar voice whispered a greeting in my ear. I wasn't sure if I was born in Egypt, but that was where many of my oldest memories lay.

I didn't have many memories of our time in Egypt. I had forgotten the numerous occasions we had been in love, where he claimed to remember every single one of them—eight in total. But I doubted that in this moment, in the comfort of the dream. Because, in reality, I hadn't seen or heard from him in weeks. But every night when I closed my eyes, he was there. Holding me. Kissing me. Painting me. Loving me.

"Good morning, my love," he'd said in a language older than Egypt itself.

He'd loved me then, before the pyramids were built. I knew it for the truth as sure as I knew the words he'd whispered in my ear. I rested in his embrace as I watched history rise around me.

We were on the island of Philae where the

Temple of Isis sat. This temple was one of many built for the goddess. Philae was near Greece. The goddess, Isis, was highly favored and devoutly revered in the Egyptian, Greek, and Roman cultures.

Time sped up as the temple rose before us, piece by piece. The sun and moon arced across the sky as I turned in the crescent of Zane's body.

"Zane?"

"*Oui, ma petite nova?*"

"I miss you."

"You have me, *mon coeur*. You have always had me. You will always have me."

I turned into his body, resting my forehead against his lips, my hands against his broad shoulders. In his arms, I couldn't remember why I was angry with him. Why I was alone in a bed at this very moment and not curled up with him.

He'd only tried to protect me, to keep me safe. Okay, so yeah, maybe he didn't tell me some things from our shared past that came back to bite me in the ass a couple of millennia later. But I had secrets of my own.

His fingers traced my cheekbones. Even in my dreams, he sought out the details of my body to use in his artwork. I held still for him as I always did, allowing him to love me through the expression of his art.

The sounds of children laughing filled my ears, and my heart sank as the reasons why I had turned from this man flooded into my head. This gentle man had committed genocide in my name. The ghoulish details came back as the blood of the Lin Kuie men, women, and children filled my vision.

I pulled away and peered into his face, unchanged for millennia. His skin was deeply tanned from lying on Mediterranean sands. His eyes were dark, hooded by long lashes that covered the secrets he still held. One lock of his thick, curly hair fell forward as it always did. I balled my fingers into a fist instead of reaching for it. I stared at him and tried to see the evil in him. He held still and let me look my fill.

And like the last time I'd seen him, my heart had trouble reconciling what my mind knew. That was likely why I had forgotten it the first time. I wished I could forget again so I could close my eyes and get lost in his arms, his kiss, his body. But the battle raged inside me. So loud was my indecision that it took on a voice.

The sounds of the children turned to chants. They were rhythmic and lulling. A drumbeat started, and then a voice emerged from the beat. That had never happened since I'd been dreaming these dreams of my past with Zane over the last few weeks.

"Nia," someone called.

I turned and saw a woman. She was dressed in a peplos from ancient times. Her light hair flowed around her. She seemed tall, too tall to be human. Even though she was surrounded by children, she looked as though she were a giant.

"Nia." She beckoned me.

I hesitated to leave the comfort and familiarity of Zane's presence, but when I turned back to him, he was gone. My heartbeat sped up as I glanced around. My eyes wildly searched when I couldn't find him.

"Nia."

I wrenched my eyes open to a blonde woman with blue eyes.

"Dreaming about Fine Frenchie again?" Loren asked as she hovered over me.

"What? No." I turned from Loren, hiding my face as I came fully awake.

"You should call him."

I shook my head as I rolled over and got out of the bed.

"Then call Broody Billionaire."

I nearly tripped at the thought of her new suggestion. Tresor Mohandis was someone else I wasn't prepared to see or even think about. But I knew Loren wouldn't let this bone go so easily. So I turned the tables around on her.

"Let's talk about your ex instead," I said.

"My ex? You mean Lenny the demon. You think he sold his soul to the devil?"

"We think that's how it works. No one knows for sure."

Or if they did, they didn't share. Immortals weren't always forthcoming with information. For beings who lived longer than recorded time, money was no object. Our currency was information and memories of times gone past.

"I wonder how much he got for it?" Loren's eyes went unfocused, the way they did when she was thinking of doing something less than savory. "What do you think a soul goes for these days?"

"I doubt he got any actual currency. The exchange is for long life and strength. I assume the human has to make something of that himself."

"What does the devil get? An army? Minions? To what end?"

"Power is a drug."

We'd seen that with the leader of the Gongyi

tribe who'd led us to the dragon bone. During our adventures in China, Mr. Xu had been a man so driven by the need to advance his family that he'd gone mad and was prepared to murder those who got in the way of his plan. Instead of advancing his family, they'd been once again wiped off the face of the planet, save a few who were under constant observation.

"Do you think the blond flasher is the devil incarnate?" Loren asked, bringing me back to our present adventure.

"I don't know," I said. "Maybe." But even as I said the words, I knew they weren't right. But what was he if not an Immortal? Definitely not a knight. A wizard, maybe?

"Well . . ." Loren said. "He sure remembers you."

I glared at Loren. She grinned back. She had never cowered under my displeasure or my daggers. She had too much estrogen for cowardice.

"I can't remember who he is," I admitted. "But I'm sure we've met before."

"Do you think you were lovers?"

"I don't know." I cringed. I hid my face in my hands, feeling like a loose woman. "But I am pretty sure he's the one in charge. He saw me come in. He knew what I was, so he knows I don't have a soul to take. What we need to figure out is why they want you?"

"Because I'm awesome," Loren said.

"You're also a criminal mastermind."

She gasped, placing her hand over her heart. "That has to be the nicest thing you've ever said about me."

When she wasn't out raiding tombs for treasure, Loren had spent much of her life making . . . shall we say, imitation art.

"What was Baros into when you two were together?"

Loren shrugged. "Anything that gave him a kick of adrenaline. Mostly, he was a fighter—boxing, Muay Thai, any type of competition fighting. He was my sword master while my dad was consulting on the restoration of the Parthenon. Meanwhile, I was a teenager hot for teacher."

"He didn't take advantage of you, did he?"

Loren snorted.

I realized it was a stupid question. She likely took full advantage of him.

"He wouldn't touch me until I came of age," she confirmed. "I tracked him down as soon as I turned eighteen."

"He has the build of a gladiator."

"Oh yeah, he does." She waggled her eyebrows. "Wait!" Her brows shot up. "So Lenny could be hundreds of years old. He could be an actual gladiator. Like, I banged Russell Crowe."

It was possible. I looked down at the ancient ring I still coveted.

"But if he's super human," Loren said, "that means when we were risking our necks bungee jumping and rock climbing, he wasn't in much danger while I was actually risking my sweet life?"

I nodded.

"The asshole. And I thought he cared."

I shrugged.

"So, demons are strong, they live forever, and they have no pupils. Anything else?"

"I haven't run into many of them—not for hundreds of years. Most of them seem to keep to Europe and Greece."

Greece. That was another place I didn't visit often. I'd assumed it was because of things I was trying to forget. Things like my time there with Tresor Mohandis. But now I wondered if something else had happened.

"There are devils and demons in the world?" Loren asked. "Do you think they drank your blood or bones in the past? Because it sure looked like

Golden Rod had free access to your body at one point in time."

I threw a pillow at her. She caught it instead of ducking.

I aimed a warning finger. "I just want to point out that whatever and whomever I do in my lifetime, you will always be Top Ho."

"You're so magnanimous to give me the crown." Loren stood and inclined her head regally. "Are we gonna go to this mystery party in Greece or what?"

"Let's see if we can get more information on these demons and—what did you call him?—Golden Rod, first. I know someone who may know more about demons, especially if they have anything to do with Greece."

CHAPTER FIVE

We touched down in Turkey later the next day. It was Loren's first time in Istanbul. She strained her neck looking at the Byzantine domes, golden minarets, and grand courtyards. I left her to sightsee while I headed off on my family reunion.

The city had changed since I'd been here over a hundred years ago. After invaders came into the country from each side, after countless wars, after thirty-six sultans, the West had finally infiltrated the East as evidenced in the crossroads of the marketplace I walked through to get to my destination.

The call to prayer sounded from the loudspeakers of a mosque announcing the midday prayer. Not everyone stopped their work and headed to the mosque or dropped to their knees in salat. Women walked around with their heads uncovered, showing off fashionable hairstyles and made-up faces. Men held phones to their ears and continued to do business instead of dropping their heads in prayer.

Istanbul had been the imperial capital of the Byzantium empire, then it became the conquered city of Constantinople, and was now the largest city of the republic, which now held a constitution. The city, which had once been the center of the stronghold that had conquered large swaths of Asia, Europe, and Africa, was no longer the capital of the great nation. That was something I knew chaffed its longtime political architect.

Bet had been pulling the strings of human puppets since recorded time. The Ottoman Empire had been a pet project of his beginning as far back as his days with the Mongolian Horde that had swept across the Eastern hemisphere. He had been whispering in the ears of khans and sultans and, even more recently, presidents. His huns, sultans, and caliphs had stretched their rule far and wide for centuries, bringing what was once a small Anatolian tribe to rule some of the greatest cultures in history

—until a man with modern ideas put the brakes on Bet's progress.

After the First World War, Ataturk, regarded as the Father of Turkey, put an end to the Ottoman dynasty and issued reforms that ended the monastic way of life. Ataturk introduced representation for the people. He instituted parliament and participatory democracy—all of which were anathema to Bet.

Bet had recently returned from America, where he'd been instrumental in installing the country's newest president—a firebrand whose speech called to days long past where the wealthy and privileged were the ruling class and had all the power.

I walked down the halls of Bet's home. There was no security, just assistants. Though Bet had more than his fair share of enemies, there wasn't much a human could do to him other than put a kink in his plans. But Bet always played the long game. In time, whatever seeds he'd sown in the Western world would come to bear fruits that would enhance the bounty on his table.

I felt the prickle as I got closer to the closed door he must be behind. Bet was old. His name, and the brand on his back, marked him as the second oldest Immortal.

When I opened the door, Bet sat lounging at his desk with a crystal tumbler in his hand. His dark beard was trim along his square jaw. His shoulders were as broad as a warrior's in his fitted businessman's suit. Light gray eyes sat out against his toasty, warm skin.

He was handsome by any culture or time period's standards. But behind that sultry gaze, his mind was always calculating, adding up how to get the best of his opponents. And, yes, everyone he encountered was an opponent in his eyes.

My body was framed in the doorway, and his gaze locked on mine, pinning me at the threshold. I rolled my shoulders and pressed my shoulder blades into my spine to relieve some of the pressure that had gathered. Immortals became allergic when in one another's presence for an extended period. The awareness of one another was immediate, hence the prickle in my throat. But the more sinusy effects could take days, weeks to manifest. Unless more than one of us were gathered together at the same time.

After only a few seconds of standing in the doorway, my nose twitched. The corners of my eyes watered. Bet was old, but he shouldn't have such an effect on me.

His brow raised as he regarded me, seemingly unaffected. He didn't rise from his chair. "I would say that this is a surprise, Tisa, but you were expected."

"Was I?" I asked, coming further into the room.

"Yes, we were just talking about you." Bet inclined the glass tumbler in his hand to the corner of the room.

My hand instinctively went to my hip for my blade. In the never-ending battle of fight or flight, my response was always fight. When I saw who it was, my fingers froze and my feet itched to flee.

Tresor Mohandis leaned against a bookshelf. His honey-golden skin stretched across defined biceps that were crossed at his chest. Through the V of his white cotton shirt, I saw more tanned skin with dips and peaks that brought my mind to the dangerous dunes of a desert. My mouth went parched, and I felt beads of sweat forming at my brow as though I were in a heatwave.

Tres's dark gaze raked my body, making me feel as though I was caught in a sandstorm that the fabric covering me could not withstand. I felt naked, exposed, and in dire need of a strong, stiff drink.

"Dr. Rivers."

"Hi." My voice was breathy, like a young girl facing off with her crush. Tres's formal address, along with his unexpected presence, caught me off guard. I cleared my throat and began again. This time, with command in my voice. "What are you doing here?"

"Likely the same thing you are," Tres said. "Alerting the others about the Lin Kuie."

Oh. Right. The old bad guys. I was on to the next bad guys.

"What's going on?" Tres asked, taking a step toward me.

His molten eyes bored into me, seeing things I didn't want him to, things I couldn't remember. There had been a time when we'd been close. I may have loved him once. I knew he used to love me. But I couldn't remember.

That wasn't true.

I might not remember the details, but I did remember what it felt like to be in his arms, to have his lips pressed against mine, to be in his care and under his protection.

"Have you gotten yourself in more trouble since the last time I saw you?" he asked.

"Trouble?" I parroted.

Tres grinned, and I gulped. I had grown so used to Tresor Mohandis frowning or growling at me over the last few hundred years. When he grinned, it made my knees weak. It brought out the breathiness in my voice.

"What have you done now, Theta?" he asked, his voice low.

The Grecian word brought me back to why I was here. "Demons."

Tres quirked an eyebrow.

I turned back to Bet. Mostly to come out from under the assault of Tres's hypnotic gaze. It worked. My wits came back to me with a force that knocked sense into my clouded head.

Unlike the grinning man in the corner, Bet's jaw was locked as he leaned back in his chair. His gaze was on his drink. But that calm nonchalance was a mask. Bet's light eyes were focused. He was calculating.

"I had a run-in with some demons a couple of nights ago," I said.

"You were in Greece?" Tres asked.

"No, Budapest."

Bet's head rose. His eyes sharpened on me. It was Bet who had first told me about demons.

It had been some time after the great Battle of Thermopylae. Much of today's society believed the battle between the small band of Greek Spartans and the vast and plentiful Persian army had been decided at the narrow coastal pass over three days of a bare-chested, spear-thrusting, shield-wielding battle. When in truth, the battle had been won in the Straits of Artemisium. Many of the Greek forces that had blocked the Persian navy had been without pupils. Bet still hadn't gotten over that embarrassing defeat by a demon army to this day.

"What were slaves doing in Budapest?" Bet asked. His free hand balled into a fist, as though he were preparing to grab one of the spears off the wall behind him and race to Hungary for a fight.

"Having an orgy," I said.

Bet shook his head in disgust. I opened my mouth to ask more questions, but a deep voice filled the room.

"What were you doing at an orgy?" Tres asked.

My lips flapped for an answer before I remembered he wasn't the boss of me and I didn't owe him one. I turned back to Bet. "I was trying to track down information on the Eleusinian Mysteries. It's a cult that's said to grant its followers everlasting life. There had been a tablet in the possession of the Greek Ministry of Culture—the Ninnion Tablet. It was said to illustrate the ritual, but it disappeared years ago."

"And you thought it would be at a sex party?" Tres sounded incredulous.

I wasn't sure I liked his tone. "My associate, Ms. Van Alst—"

"The blonde tomb raider?" Tres interrupted yet again.

"She had a contact who offered her an invitation to the Eleusinian Mystery rituals. The contact, it turned out, was a demon. She didn't know the signs, but I did. His eyes were black, pupil-less."

"Was there red around the rims?" Bet asked. He'd set his glass down and balled his other fist. His eyes were no longer sharp. They were clouded with fury.

"Um, no."

Bet sighed. "Then he wasn't a demon. He was Chosen." His hands relaxed, and he slumped back in his chair.

There was that word again. "What's a Chosen?"

Bet ignored me, rubbing at the whiskers on his chin. I watched as the fury receded from his eyes and his pupils twitched in calculation.

In the corner of the room, Tres smiled. Actually, gloated was more like it. Was he thrilled to know something I didn't?

I was starting to realize that neither man looked

particularly shocked by these revelations. It would make sense that Immortals and demons, or Chosen, had run into each other over the centuries. But since my kind didn't have family reunions or an Immortal group chat, we didn't always share the information we'd gathered about the world. Unless it was something that affected us as a whole.

"Were there only Chosen and humans at this party?" Bet asked.

"What else would there be?" I asked.

"Humans have pupils, Chosen don't. Was there anyone whose eyes … sparkled?"

Did he mean Golden Rod? "Yes, there was a blond man. It looked like his eyes … This may sound …"

As Immortals, we'd seen our fair share of bizarre things take place. But I still felt weird talking about seeing a bolt of lightning in a man's eyes. Luckily, Bet said it for me.

"There was lightning in his eyes?" he asked.

I nodded.

Bet cursed under his breath. "What's his angle in Hungary? They're landlocked and their economy is export-driven."

"What are you talking about?" I asked, but Bet paid me no heed as he continued planning his attack. Bet saw everything and everyone as a threat to the power he sought to gain in the world. "He knew me. He insinuated that we had a . . . relationship."

They both looked at me. There was judgment in Bet's eyes. Tres's were carefully blank. I felt like the girl who'd blacked out at the party and was asking who had her panties the next morning.

"Who is he?" I asked.

"You don't remember?" Tres sounded cautious.

This was one of the reasons we didn't do family reunions. Other families competed over what accomplishments each member had. Mine competed over what was remembered or forgotten.

"If I remembered, I wouldn't have come here asking questions," I said, the irritation thick in my throat.

"What do you want to know?" Tres asked.

I decided I didn't want Tres to tell me anything about Golden Rod. If something had happened between golden boy and me, I'd rather it stay in the dark. But I did need to know more about these pupil-less humans.

"These demons, or Chosen," I said, "how are they made? Did we have anything to do with it?"

"Do you mean did a demon murder and drink

the bones of an Immortal?" Tres snorted, his face softening from its blank composure. "No. Their souls are taken."

"Their souls aren't taken," Bet said. "They are sacrificed."

"To who?" I asked.

"The gods," Bet answered.

I felt a chill run down my back. I knew this part of the story. But the pages were blurry in my mind.

"At least they call themselves gods," Bet spat. He picked up his tumbler. Then, noticing it was empty, he slammed it down.

"What are they?" I asked. "Who are they?"

"They are abominations," Bet answered. "And their intent is to spread their disease amongst humanity and take over the world."

Tres rolled his eyes. "They're not trying to take over the world. They keep to Greece. I think they draw their power from the land as much as they do from the people. Sometimes they venture into Europe and America, but not for long."

"For now," Bet said. "But that bastard was in Hungary."

"At a party," Tres replied. "Do you think he's planning a military attack through an orgy?"

Bet turned and gave us his back. His head tilted

up to the collection of weapons on his wall. Though Bet was a cunning strategist, he wasn't afraid to get his hands dirty. He'd fought beside Sultan Suleyman the Magnificent, who had spread his empire to . . . Greece.

I hadn't noticed how often Bet seemed to have his hand in the battles to overtake the Greek State. I'd also never seen Bet so agitated. This man had led armies without so much as an eye twitch. He manipulated the world's most powerful men and women until they were wrapped around his fingers, doing bidding they didn't even understand, might never see the true outcome of in their lifetime. Bet was ancient, often cruel, and completely single-minded.

As I looked at him now, his jaw clenched. His eyes were unfocused and twitching. His nostrils flared like a cornered beast.

"Excuse me," I said. "Who are these people, or gods, or whatever?"

Tres and Bet turned back to me, as though they'd forgotten I was there.

"I can't believe you forgot this." Tres had a huge, amused grin on his handsome face. "Now I don't feel so affronted that you forgot us. You and she used to be very close."

"Me and who?" I asked.

"That bitch has been trying to use Tisa to get to me for centuries." Bet snarled. His eyes were wide, his arms crossed over his chest. He paced the floor with shuffled steps.

"You think everything is about you," Tres said dismissively.

"It usually is," Bet countered.

"Hello . . ." I waved my arms. "Who are you talking about? What bitch?"

Tres opened his mouth to answer, but Bet rounded his desk and grabbed the other man's shoulder.

"Don't say her name," Bet said. "Any mention fuels the empty vessel that she is."

Tres shrugged off Bet's grip and faced me. "Demeter."

Bet groaned, running his hands through his hair and messing up his orderly locks.

"Demeter?" I asked.

"Yeah, Demeter," Tres parroted.

"Enough." Bet cut the empty air with the straight edge of his hand.

"As in the Greek goddess?" I asked.

Tres nodded, a twinkle in his dark eyes.

"She's not . . . Is she real?"

His smile widened. "Very much so. And you two were friends once. I wonder what she did to make you forget her?"

I wondered, too.

"If you want to open this can of worms," Bet said, "you go right on ahead. But don't drag me back into that family's craziness. I tried to bring civilization to that corner of the world for centuries, but they insist on being a den of heathens as they take more and more souls to march in their cause."

"They have no cause but to live," Tres said.

"For them to live, they need to eat souls." Bet looked disgusted. "They're a threat to our existence."

And with that, Bet, the Sultan of Cool, the King of Khans, the Iago of Presidents, marched out of the room. The man who had felled hordes and militias looked as though he was frightened by the mention of the name Demeter.

Who was this woman?

CHAPTER SIX

"Nia, wait up," Tres called as he ran after me.

With our host departing in a huff, and few answers to my questions, I'd left Bet's home shortly after he'd left the room, leaving Tres standing in the corner. I may have left rather quickly, with my legs pumping a bit faster than a walk. It wasn't like I was running away from anything, or anyone.

"Slow down, would you?"

I took a deep breath and slowed my pace. It wasn't like he couldn't catch me. It was just that I wasn't sure I wanted to get caught. By him.

Breaking up with Zane was still a raw and ragged scar in my chest. And Tres had made it crystal clear the last time I'd seen him that he wanted to pick up where we'd left off a millennium ago. I still remembered the lingering kiss he'd whispered upon my lips the last time I'd seen him. It had awakened something inside me that I'd been trying to put back to sleep ever since.

I closed my eyes as I paused in the market outside Bet's place. My nose twitched as Tres drew closer, but I focused on the smell of food in the air. The sounds of a large crowd gathered outside wafted to my ears. I opened my eyes to see people sitting patiently with untouched food laid out before them.

It was Ramadan, and the city's inhabitants were coming together to break their fast. They'd spent the day keeping themselves from bad habits and evil thoughts, making a sacrifice to their God. Though the sun was setting, the fast wasn't truly broken until the evening call for prayers.

My stomach grumbled at the delicious smells. I hadn't eaten since leaving Loren this morning. I was starving. The pangs of hunger, of emptiness, of needing to be filled slammed into me.

I felt Tres at my back. He stood silently, but his gaze upon me was loud. He was probably just as hungry as I was. It would be polite to ask him out to dinner so we both could see to our basic needs. But I didn't. Though I wasn't Muslim, it was impolite to eat in front of everyone before the fast was broken. Dinner would have to wait.

"Well, that's new," I said, breaking the heavy silence between us.

"What?"

His deep voice rumbled through me, and I shuddered. In an effort to hide the tremor that coursed through my body, I turned around to face him. That was a mistake. His gaze pinned me, and my stomach grumbled. I coughed to cover the sound. I looked away, losing focus in the crowd.

"Bet," I said. "I've never seen him lose his cool."

Tres shrugged. "He and Demeter have a bit of a past."

"Really?" I turned to Tres with interest. I assumed when he said *past,* he meant it in the biblical sense, and of biblical proportions. Of course, Bet had had his share of affairs. He was a powerful, rich, and handsome man. But I'd never known him to have a *past* with a woman.

"Greece was under Ottoman rule for over four hundred years," Tres pointed out.

"Yeah, I know."

"The sultans battled hard to keep control of that little piece of the world. You ever wonder why?"

"Same stupid reasons as always—territory,

resources, freedom. Or the infidels were worshipping the wrong gods. Or the most common reason—because those savages who are different from us are evil."

Tres smiled and shook his head. "There's another, more common, stupider reason."

I frowned as I racked my brain for an alternative answer. Only one other option remained, and it was unfathomable. "No way," I said.

Tres nodded, a huge grin lighting his face.

"Really?" I breathed, leaning in and whispering as though it were a great secret.

"Truly." Tres chuckled.

I couldn't believe it. The other stupid reason that men went to war was love. But Bet? My curiosity was piqued.

Tres's handsome features rearranged themselves into something more boyish. I couldn't help but stare. Soon, the boyish grin faded and the curl of a man's mouth stepped into its place. I looked away, turning my attention to Bet and his War of the Roses with his paramour.

"Tell me about her," I said. "This goddess Demeter."

"You knew her better than I did. And she didn't prefer *me* with you."

"Who did she—"

The darkening of his gaze shut me up. I knew which Immortal my forgotten BFF, Demeter, preferred. "Well, if it's any consolation, Loren is totes Team Broody Billionaire."

"Totes team what?"

"It doesn't matter." I shook my head, not wanting to let him know that not only did we have a nickname for him, but we also talked about him like girls hanging out in the bathroom at the school dance.

Tres and I stood close, but there was a gulf of tension between our bodies. Out before us, a group of men in tall, fuzzy top hats and dark clothes took center stage. The clothing identified them as Whirling Dervishes—followers of the ancient philosopher, Rumi.

Rumi taught tolerance, love, and the liberation of women—radical ideas that caused his sect to never be accepted by Orthodox Islam. Along with these beliefs, the Dervishes had another practice that was unpalatable—they danced.

Rumi and his followers believed the union with God could be achieved through dance. Music notes filled the air. The Dervishes shed their cloaks, casting aside their earthly ties. The men raised their right hands to receive the blessings of the divine. They lowered their left hands to distribute those blessings down to earth. And then, they began to spin.

"Broody?" Tres's deep voice rumbled down through the cone of my ear.

I took a deep breath to stave off the shudder. Then I looked up at him. "Well, you do have the scowl down."

And then he went and smiled. The lifting of his lips reminded me of the mischief of a little boy mixed with the devilish knowledge of a grown man.

"Do you like the scowl?" he asked. His face was soft. Those dark eyes twinkled under the fading light of the setting sun.

He was flirting. Tresor Mohandis flirting with me was a force I didn't know how to reckon with. Thankfully, I was saved by the bell. Or rather, the song.

The sound of singing filled the air. It was the call to prayer. The people gathered around raised their hands in supplication. When the evening prayer was done, they broke bread and began to eat. Which then reminded me of my unfulfilled hunger and the rumbling that had migrated from my belly southward.

I turned from the festivities toward the mosque. It was the Rustem Pasha Mosque. It was empty since everyone was out in the marketplace breaking their fast. I felt Tres behind me as I entered. It felt like I was prey and he was stalking me, playing with his food before he pounced and devoured his quarry whole.

"Are you waiting for me to give you an answer?" I asked, bringing the conversation back to whether I liked his scowl.

"No need." His deep voice echoed off the mosaic walls of the mosque's interior. "The fact that you keep running away from me is answer enough."

I turned. It was foolish to put my back against the wall to such a worthy adversary. Especially when his body would block my exit. But the route to the exit was free and clear. Tres leaned against a wall nowhere near me or the doorway. Still, his presence filled the room.

The allergy no longer bothered me. It was only him, and we'd only been alone for a few minutes. But I still felt the prickles all over my skin.

I relaxed my stance, but not my guard. "I know I haven't called."

"Because you're back with him."

"No."

"No?"

I ran my fingers over the blue tiles of the church walls. The color was turquoise. Turkish blue. Turquoise. Huh? French and Turkish made blue. I turned from the tiles and faced Tres.

"I haven't seen Zane since . . ." I swallowed hard. Then I closed my eyes to the memory.

After the nightmare of the Gongyi with the Lin Kuie, I'd gone to find Zane in the South of France at the cottage we'd gone to when we'd fallen in love. He'd waited there for me. We'd argued. Well, I'd argued. He'd taken my ire as his due. Then, once all the fight had gone out of me, there'd been none left to fight for us. He'd left me alone. My chin wobbled at the memory of opening my eyes to find him gone.

"I'm sorry," Tres murmured. He was still behind me, but his voice sounded closer. Then I felt his breath on my ear. "I made an assumption. Breakups are hard, I know."

After Tres and I had broken up a thousand years ago, we'd gone to war with each other. As a land developer and an architect, Tres had a nasty habit of building on historic sites I wanted to excavate. Problem was, there wasn't much untouched, viable land left on this earth, which meant that just about everywhere had some historic significance to someone or other.

We'd had our own War of the Roses for hundreds of years. I just hadn't realized ours wasn't over control of land. It was over heartbreak that I'd banished from memory.

I used to think him a heartless tyrant. As I looked at him now, leaning casually against the wall, he looked like a gentle giant. No, check that. He looked like a dark panther toying with his meal before pouncing.

"You're thrilled Zane and I are apart," I said. "Now you can make your move."

He didn't move. Tres ran his hands across the mosaic tile, just beside mine. Our fingers were close. He could reach out and grab me. But he didn't.

"Did you know I built this mosque?" he asked.

"You did not. Mimar Sinan built it back in the sixteenth century."

"He designed it. I built it. It's beautiful, isn't it?"

I looked at the arching domes. The work was exquisite. The colorful patterns and geometric shapes were hypnotic. They urged people to stare, to tilt their head further back and marvel until the blood drained and left them dizzy.

"I don't just tear things down," Tres said. "I'm capable of making something beautiful."

I ran my hands over the mosaic patterns, still steering clear of his fingertips. The colors between us were blue and a light red that looked like . . . "Fuck weasel."

"Pardon?"

"Nothing." I dropped my hand from the wall. I had no intention of explaining to Tres the inside joke about autocorrect and colors that Zane and I shared.

"Are you headed to Greece?" he asked. "To find Demeter?"

"Yeah." I nodded. "Loren and I are probably gonna catch a flight out early tomorrow morning."

I needed to check on her. It wasn't only because I didn't want to stay here under his gaze, which was making my heart skip beats. Loren was likely wreaking havoc during the holy hour somewhere.

"I'm headed there," Tres said. "To Greece. I can give you a lift."

I tried to shake my head to decline his offer. Instead, I stared at his gleaming teeth under the light of the dome. I had the sensation that this man could eat me alive if I let him get too close. He took a step forward. I couldn't step back. My back was against the wall.

"I'm sailing," he said. "You like boats, if I remember."

Sailing was one of my great joys. But I kept my mouth shut. I wrapped my hands around the pillar against my back. There was a dagger at my hip, but I didn't feel the need to reach for it as he advanced. It would've been ineffectual against the assault he was putting into place against me.

"I have a yacht," he said. "What if I let you take the wheel?"

"Why? What do you want from me?"

"Why do you suppose anyone offering you a hand has an ulterior motive?"

I quirked an eyebrow. "Trust issues."

Tres's grin spread. "Then let me be clear: I want to spend time with you. During that time, I plan to demonstrate many of my great character traits to entice your interest in having me as a sexual partner."

"Oh . . . that was . . . a thorough explanation."

"I like clarity in all things," he said.

He was standing toe to toe with me now. One more inch and he'd brush my blade. But he held himself back.

"Is sleeping with you the cost of passage?" I had intended to put snark in my voice but failed. Again, it came out breathy.

Tres chuckled. His breath sailed across my lips. "No. The ride is free. I won't sleep with you."

Was that disappointment at the center of my chest?

"Not on this passage," he said. "I have very definite designs for you, Theta. First, I'll lay a solid foundation by wining and dining you. I'll impress you with witty conversation and stories of my accomplishments that show off my impressive intellect and expertise. You know, we used to call that courting in another time. Then I'll build the tension between us, brick by brick, until I reach your pinnacle. That's when I'll stake my flag. And trust me when I tell you, when you come to my bed, we won't be sleeping."

My stomach was in knots. My thighs were squeezed together. Both my hands were balled in fists. He was so close to me. He only needed to lean down an inch and his lips would meet mine. But he pulled away.

"So, Dr. Rivers, can I take you for a ride?"

CHAPTER SEVEN

"**I**'m king of the world."

Loren stood at the helm of the yacht as it pulled away from the Turkish port. Her feet were hooked on the railing and her arms were thrown wide. She could've easily fallen over and into the depths. It might not kill her, but it would certainly injure her.

"Loren," I called. "Get down from there."

"One more minute, Mom." She flung her head back and let the wind catch her blonde locks as the ship picked up speed. "Near . . . far . . . wherever you—*oh*!"

She wobbled, and I grabbed for her. She landed in my arms like a damsel swooning. Only difference was the bag slung over her shoulder with a deadly weapon in its belly. The cane that sheathed a sword dug into my ribs.

"See what I mean?" I admonished. "I told you to be careful."

"I was fine," she insisted as I held her aloft in my arms. "Why, Dr. Rivers, I declare. I've never been quite so swept off my feet."

I rolled my eyes at her. She grinned as I set her on the ground.

"I knew it," she said. "You *do* have a girl crush on me."

I gave her a shove, but she only laughed at my rejection. Contrary to her belief, I didn't have a crush on her. But I had gotten used to her presence over the last couple of months. I would've dove in and fished her out of the water. That was also because she was wearing my vintage jeans.

Being an Immortal was a lonely lifestyle. I'd had human companions before. Some I was close to, others I wasn't, most I'd forgotten. It was hard watching people I cared about grow old and die while I remained forever unchanged physically but mentally ancient. Loren would only be around for another eighty years at best. But I had the feeling I'd remember her for the rest of my endless days.

As she brushed off my jeans and straightened a

top I wasn't sure I'd lent her, a butler came up and presented us with a tray of food. There were crudités, pastries, and pomegranate seeds. Loren double-fisted a sample of each dish and gobbled them down.

"I was born for this lifestyle," she said around a mouthful of food, then promptly washed it down with the contents of the wine glass that was handed to her. The vintage, I noted, was three times her age.

"You were born the daughter of a scientist," I reminded her.

Loren frowned. "The last place I should be is in a lab with beakers and chemicals and maths."

"Is that why you traveled with your dad?"

Loren's father had been a world-renowned archaeologist. That was before he was caught forging an artifact. That artifact happened to be the reason Loren and I had met. Dr. Van Alst had found evidence of an ancient Chinese dynasty in a small, forgotten province in China—the Gongyi. Years later, his daughter had led me to the same tribe. Since then, our paths had remained interwoven.

"Loren, you never told me about your mother."

Loren gulped down the remaining contents of the wine glass before she answered. "She died when I was young. She was English. I barely remember her." Loren continued to speak as she nibbled her food. "I traveled with my dad because none of my relatives, nor any boarding school, would have me."

"Doesn't surprise me."

"You know what doesn't surprise me? The fact you're over here talking to me instead of chatting up the Broody Billionaire over there."

Tres stood at the helm of his ship, talking to the captain of the vessel. He must've felt my gaze on him, because his head rose a second after I laid eyes on him. He smiled and nodded his head.

My gaze dipped to the floor.

"Wow." Loren's sigh was disappointed. "You are seriously bad at flirting."

"Shut up," I growled, turning to look out at the sea. "I've been in a relationship for over five hundred years. I'm just a little rusty is all."

Something splashed in the depths of the water. It looked like the tentacle of an octopus. Octopuses were common in tropical waters such as the Mediterranean, but they preferred shallow, coastal lines. We had pulled a good distance from the coast of Turkey.

I peered down into the fathomless waters. Upon further inspection, I noted that the tentacle looked a bit furry, like a bundle of hair and not tough skin. I leaned over the railing. As I squinted, it looked like the creature had more than eight tentacles, as though the octopus had a head full of furry locks.

"Do you see that?" I pointed at the waters.

"See what?" Loren peered over the railing. "I don't see anything."

"I . . ." I searched the waters and saw nothing. "Never mind."

"Nia?" Loren waited until I turned away from the water and gave her my full attention. "Flirting is all about getting someone's attention."

We were back on Tres. "I know that." I looked back into the depths of the water, but my eight-legged, hairy friend, or whatever I had seen, had gone.

"Nia?"

"What?" I turned to Loren.

Her blue gaze raked over me, looking for something. "Do you *want* Tres's attention?"

It wasn't often that Loren struck a serious tone. This was one of those rare moments. The mischief faded from her gaze, and I saw myself reflected in her eyes.

I saw uncertainty and hesitation. I also saw desire. I couldn't deny I was attracted to Tres. I couldn't deny that whatever had been between us a thousand years ago was still there. Remnants of feelings swirled around my head and chest like the steam over a piping hot cup of tea that, even after sitting on the coffee table for an hour, still hadn't entirely cooled. Even though it might have gone tepid, I knew it would still be satisfying.

I blinked and pulled my gaze back to focus on Loren's entire face. Her brows were lowered as though they'd give me a lift. Her lashes pulled together as though they'd surround me with support. Her lips were in a thin line as though she'd stand behind me in solidarity with whatever decision I made.

I had difficulty pushing the two words past my lips, so I began by nodding my head. Then the words tumbled out as though my attraction to Tres had pushed them through. "I do."

"Oh, thank God!" The cool, supportive, nonjudgmental facade melted away from Loren's face and was replaced with glee. "Because I'm supposed to live like this, Nia." She waved her hands around the massive yacht whose deck we stood upon. "And I will be the third wheel pushing you to that man if it keeps me in this lap of luxury."

"Great, Loren," I said, chuckling. "Way to be supportive."

"I am so your wingwoman. Okay, here's what you're going to do. You're going to go and talk to him. You'll tell him what a big, massive boat he has."

"That's not subtle at all."

"But you're going to change first. That shirt is far from revealing."

"Wait a minute," I said. "Did you say wingwoman or pimp?"

"Too late. Target approaching."

Loren gave me a whirl and shoved me forward. I wobbled and fell into a hard chest. Tres caught me. His hands held me by the elbows. Once he was certain I'd regained my balance, he set me back on my feet. But he didn't let me go.

"I trust you ladies have everything you need?" he asked, looking into my eyes.

I was thousands of years old, but whenever this man spoke to me, I was as tongue-tied as a schoolgirl.

"We do," Loren answered. "Nia was just commenting on how big your boat is. Maybe you should give her a tour."

"I'd love to show you around . . ." he said. His voice was silky-smooth. After a pause, he finished, ". . . my boat."

Tres gave me his arm. I took it with shaky fingers,

glancing over my shoulder at Loren. She mouthed, *Don't screw this up for me.* I rolled my eyes and began walking alongside Tres.

I couldn't shake the feeling that everything felt familiar with him. The feel of his bicep beneath my fingers. The brush of his hip against mine as we walked.

We started at the aft, the back of the boat where Loren and I had boarded only an hour ago. We'd stepped on board and were immediately greeted with a full bar and entertainment lounge area complete with plush sofas, a glass dining set, and a big-screen television.

Tres took me past a door and onto the fly bridge, where the captain greeted me with a smile. I barely spared the man a glance as I took in all the modern technology that powered the boat. I was partial to old-fashioned sailing, but I still marveled at the screens and buttons laid out behind him.

Tres and I left the deck, passing that closed door again. We took the stairs a level down. I'd already seen the low deck cabins. There were two of them, and Loren and I had each taken one. They were the height of luxury with their own en-suites and full-sized beds.

Farther back below deck were the crew cabins.

The cramped bunks made me feel sorry for the bartender, butler, and the rest of the small crew. We headed up to the main deck. When Tres bypassed the same door on the way without opening it again, I asked why.

He paused, staring at the door and then at me. "That's the master—my bedroom. Would you like to see it?"

I hesitated.

He stepped past me and opened the door to his inner sanctum. It was done in browns, golds, and whites. It reminded me of a sheik's desert palace set out here on the water. A queen-sized bed dominated the room. A briefcase was tossed haphazardly onto the center of the mattress like a lover impatiently waiting for the caress of its master. From the belly of the case, a phone rang.

"Do you have to get that?" I asked.

"Whatever it is can wait. I'd rather talk to you."

"That's refreshing. Not being at the beck and call of your phone, I mean. People nowadays keep their heads down and in their phones."

I took a breath to stop babbling. Loren was right. I was truly awful at flirting.

"They would behave differently," Tres said, "if they had something so beautiful to look at."

Oh, crap. When the hell did Tresor Mohandis become charming? The large room suddenly felt too small. I felt the walls closing in on me, urging me to slip off my clothes, push aside the briefcase, and fall into the bed. Instead, I babbled on.

"Men nowadays prefer to chat with you through their phones on apps," I said.

"Have you been searching for companionship online?"

He stood at the doorway, leaning casually against the jamb. The door remained open, but with his big body in front of the opening, it looked like I had no escape.

"No." I shook my head. "Well, this guy I met wanted to connect with me on Instagram and—" I stopped talking and took another breath. "You know what? It's not important."

"I'm not going to answer my phone," Tres said. "But you do know that this is a date?"

"I thought you were just giving an old friend a lift."

He stepped closer, moving away from the opening and leaving me space to dart out of the room to safety. I didn't move.

"Then let me be clear," he said. "I'd like to have you for dinner tonight."

"*Have* me?"

His grin spread as he continued to slowly eat up the distance between us. "We'll sit down in the lounge area on the main deck. We'll have three courses. We'll have polite dinner conversation on topics ranging from the weather to bird-watching, and perhaps we can talk a bit of sports. All of those, I think, are safe topics for us."

"Yeah," I agreed. Of course, we were limited in safe topics thanks to our past battles over land and buildings. The walls stopped pressing in on me, but now his broad shoulders stretched out in front of me. He wasn't blocking my path. I could duck around him. If I wanted to.

"There will be no phones," he continued. "No apps, no compasses."

Grown woman, ancient being that I was, I giggled. Then I shoved my hand over my trembling lips. Had he been this winsome a thousand years ago? I stretched my brain to try to remember.

"There will also be no sex," he concluded.

"Oh?"

He grinned at the disappointment in my tone. "I'm not an easy man, Dr. Rivers." He placed an affronted hand on his chest. "I'm going to make you earn it." He leaned his head down and whispered beside my ear, "And then I'm going to make you beg for it."

I tilted my head back and met his gaze in a challenge. "If you think you're going to boss me around, you've got another think coming. I don't take orders well."

There was that damn grin again, like he knew things about me that I didn't. "Dr. Rivers may not. But my Theta . . ."

He let the sentence drag. I couldn't tell if there was a period, a question mark, or an ellipsis that was meant to end his statement. He didn't stick around to clarify. He walked away, leaving me alone in his bedroom to decide for myself.

CHAPTER EIGHT

The encounter with Tres left me feeling drained. Between the unabated hunger, the heightened fight-or-flight response, and his charming offensive, not to mention that he was one of the oldest Immortals to walk the planet, which kicked up the allergic reaction, it was a lot to deal with. The internal and external conflict took its toll, and I decided to retreat to my private cabin for a midday nap.

Of course, the moment my eyes closed, I saw *him*.

Instead of a pencil or a paintbrush in his hand, Zane held a chisel. He was shirtless. Only a pair of loose tunic pants covered his strong hips and thighs. His sculpted arms hammered at the stone tablet as he chipped away at the piece of art.

My eyes fastened to the ancient number seven on his back. The marking moved as his muscles worked. He leaned in and blew away some of the dust to reveal his work.

He'd freed the image of a woman from the stone. On the woman's head, she wore a crown. In her hand, she held something that looked like a staff with an eye. I knew it was me he was freeing from the stone. It was always me. Zane had drawn me in frescos, etched me in marble, painted me on the ceilings of chapels.

In this dream, or perhaps it was a memory, he'd drawn me as the Egyptian goddess Isis, holding the Eye of Ra. I sat on a throne surrounded by my subjects, who each held something that looked like axes in their hands. Surrounding us was . . . was that wheat?

I came closer and stared over his shoulder. With his fingers, he brushed away more of the chippings to reveal my cheekbones. His fingers brushed away the dust, lingering on the curve of my right cheek. He sat back and admired his handiwork for a moment.

"Zane?"

"*Oui, ma petite nova?*" He didn't turn. He leaned

down over his work, and his fingers continued bringing my form to life in the tablet.

"How are you?"

He turned then. His dark eyes opened wide, and he grinned. I knew I was dreaming, but my heart still skipped a beat. I itched to reach out and touch him, but something held me back. Likely the reality of the man who was in pursuit of me above deck. Zane was . . . I didn't even know where he was in the present. I only knew he hadn't come after me once we parted ways.

It struck me how dependent I'd grown upon him. Even though we couldn't spend large swaths of time together, we were in constant contact. But it had been radio silence for weeks.

"You're here with me," Zane said in my dream. "I am content."

He turned back to his work, chiseling away at my chin. I looked up, expecting to see the pyramids of Giza. Instead, I saw mountains and the Hollywood Sign of modern-day Los Angeles. I turned to Zane. The tablet was gone and a steering wheel was in his hands. We were speeding down a California highway on a bright and sunny day.

Up ahead of us was a manmade shrine. It in no

way rivaled the majesty of the Egyptian temples. It was set off a paved road surrounded by young trees.

This was a memory. I remembered this day. We'd heard about a Cult of Isis in California and decided to go see for ourselves, just for fun. The people we found at the Isis Oasis were harmless. They reminded me of the flower children of the seventies, wanting to heal the earth with love under the divine feminine.

Zane and I had rented a room from them. That night, while they showed their devotion to their idol goddess, Zane worshipped my flesh in the bed of the rented room.

In the dream, I was transported back to that room. His body roved over mine as he made love to me with his hands, his words, his whole being. I remembered his lips on my breasts, on my belly. What I didn't remember was the woman standing in the corner with wheat-colored hair and golden bright eyes.

"Nia," she said. "I need you to wake up and remember."

I jerked away from Zane in the dream and woke to tangled sheets aboard the boat. The gold fixtures in the room reminded me of the woman I'd seen in my dream. It was the second time I'd seen her while I was sleeping. I racked my brain trying to figure out who she was, what she was. Was she real? Someone from my past? Someone here in the present? I didn't know any creatures that could enter dreams like that.

My first instinct was to call Zane. He knew more about me and my past than I did. But I couldn't do that. I couldn't run to him right now, especially when I no longer trusted his renditions of my past. He'd said he'd never lied to me, but he had omitted so much—and that was the same thing. When someone knew things about me that I didn't know myself, it made me feel as though I had no control over my own life.

I sat up in the bed and pulled my computer onto my lap. I couldn't exactly search *golden-haired woman who enters dreams*. After staring at the Google search field for long moments, I typed in a URL and found myself looking at a familiar website.

Zane's smiling face blinked back at me. His eyes were cast down, which wasn't hard since his lashes were so thick. He didn't often show his face. Being Immortal, he would be recognized throughout the ages as the same person who had done various amazing pieces of art. But there was a profile picture of him on his home page now.

An event notification showed that he was in Italy. It looked like he had a showing in Rome all month long. He had missed the last showing he'd scheduled to come to my rescue. The exhibition was opening next week, and there would be a gala. Rome was a few hours from Greece. Maybe I could—

The banging at the door made me close the laptop. Loren didn't wait for me to invite her in. She turned the knob and let herself in.

"I can't believe you're in bed." Loren sounded exasperated. "Alone."

I scrubbed my hands over my face and then buried my head in a pillow. It was too early to deal with her.

"Nia Rivers, I've watched you face down a ninja horde, but you're afraid to be alone with this one man?"

"I'm not afraid," I protested. "I was just tired. And he's not the reason we're here. We still have work to do."

"You have work to do. I'm trying to achieve a new standard of living."

"While I'm lying here trying to understand my

old standard of living." I pulled my head from the pillow and stared up at the ceiling. "I used to be friends with a goddess."

I knew there were demigods—humans who had gained power by some supernatural force. But they'd been born human and then later transformed, much like store-brand comic book characters. But the Greek gods, from what I remembered, were forged from beings who were older than the very world we lived in.

If I remembered my Greek mythology correctly, the Titans, the parents of the gods of Olympus, were primeval, before mankind, animals, and even the planet. The goddess Gaia birthed the earth and her brother-husband, Uranus, birthed the sky. The two gods had children. Among them were Cronus and Rhea. Those two made another sibling-marriage and birthed the Olympians, which included Demeter, the goddess of the harvest and . . . wheat.

"Do you think Demeter created you?"

I turned my attention to Loren. "What? No. I mean, I doubt it. I have my pupils. Plus, Immortals have always believed we didn't have souls."

It was postulated that there was a spark that created life. Some scientists pointed to the fusion that happened when a sperm penetrated an egg. There were those who took that theory further and pointed to that spark as the fuel of life. No Immortal remembered their parents, which was the only thing we pointed to that indicated we potentially had no souls. But perhaps that was wrong? Perhaps this Demeter, who had figured out a way to grant immortality to humans, knew more about our origins?

"Bet said speaking her name gives her power," I said.

"What?" Loren sounded bemused. "You mean like in *Beetlejuice*?"

I'd learned that much of Loren's knowledge was garnered through books and pop culture. *Beetlejuice* was a movie about ghosts. If the name of one particular ghost, Beetlejuice, was said three times, then he'd appear and wreak havoc on that person's life.

We looked at each other.

"Demeter," Loren said slowly. And then, rapidly, "Demeter, Demeter."

We huddled on the bed, looking around the room. But nothing happened. No goddess appeared out of thin air. The ship didn't rock. The skies didn't open. We turned back to each other in disappointment. It had been a silly idea.

"Look," Loren said, "we'll deal with the Greek goddess when we get to Greece. Right now, there's a flesh-and-blood man on deck who is interested in you. I'm not just pushing you toward him because he has a boat . . . and a plane . . . and a fleet of cars and homes all over the world." She waved her hand in the air as though she were brushing Tres's many luxuries away. "I'm pushing you toward him because he's the one pursuing you."

As opposed to Zane, who was off in Rome pursuing his art career. He hadn't even tried to call or text or see me. This had been the longest we'd gone without contact in over a hundred years. But Tres wanted to go on a date with me. Tonight.

I sighed. "All right. Help me get dressed."

"To do that we're going to need my wardrobe, not yours." Loren moved the laptop out of my lap. The top flipped open before I could grab it from her.

"Loren, wait." I reached for the laptop, but she hopped out of my grasp with it in her hands.

"Why? What do you have open on here? Porn? Something like, *Indiana Jones and the Temple of Do Me?*" She opened the laptop and her smile turned into a grimace.

"I was just . . ." I started. "I was checking . . ." I gave up the pretense as Zane's face shone big on the display screen.

Loren sighed, then she shrugged. "I get it. I've been there. Lenny is my refrigerator."

"What?"

"You know, a refrigerator relationship?"

She made what I thought was a lewd motion with her hands.

"To move a fridge," Loren began, "you can't do it in one go. Well, unless you're a super-strong body builder or have Immortal powers. But my point is, normal people, we have to rock a fridge back and forth a couple of times before it'll move."

She made the motion again, which I now realized was meant to be a rocking motion, not something else.

"Zane is your refrigerator. Not surprising. The two of you are as codependent as a freezer and a fridge."

"I'm not going back to him. I've been back to him eight times. There has to be a reason I keep leaving."

"I'm not trying to get back with Lenny either. Been there, done that, more than once." Loren shrugged again. "But the best way to get over your old man—"

"I'm not getting underneath Tres."

"Of course not." Loren frowned. "You're a modern woman. You'll get on top of him, of course."

I burst out laughing and let her lead me next door.

"Now, let's get you dressed for seduction."

CHAPTER NINE

The moon shone brightly on the waters of the Mediterranean. The sea was a study in blues. During the sunlight, dark shades of cobalt flickered between turquoise and periwinkle. Mixed in with the waters was a sea of debris. The Mediterranean was one of the most polluted bodies of water on the planet.

I looked over the railing from the aft of the boat. With my keen sight, I could see deep into the water. A tendril poked above the surface. I jerked back. That was decidedly not an octopus tentacle. In this light, it looked more like a snake.

I peered down again. Two crystal blue eyes stared back at me. Then I saw an aquiline nose, and then a cruel mouth that kicked up into a grin.

"Nia?"

I jerked back, turning to Tres.

"Is everything all right?"

I turned back out to the waters. The octopus face was gone. I gripped the rail with unsteady fingers. Was I losing my mind? First floating women in my dreams and now winking sea creatures during my waking hours.

I turned as Tres came up to me. His dark eyes took me in, further unsettling my senses. He reached out a hand, indicating I should take it. I hated that I hesitated, but I did—and for good reason. The moment our skin touched, I felt a spark zip through me. It made me doubt that Immortals were soulless, not with a zap of energy like that.

He led me to the set table, then took his seat after I was settled. The first course was served and eaten in mostly silence. Though it was an amiable silence.

"How is your dish?" he asked.

We sat out on the deck of his yacht, docked in the middle of the sea between Turkey and Greece. He'd dropped anchor to steal this moment for our date.

"It's delicious," I said. "My compliments to your chef."

"Thank you." His grin was wide.

I studied his face, trying to catch his meaning.

Then my eyes widened with incredulity. "You? You made this?"

He nodded, dabbing his dinner napkin to the corners of his mouth and failing to hide his smirk.

"I didn't take you for a cook," I said.

"We weren't always well-off with humans to serve us."

Tell me about it. Whoever tailored his clothing had outdone themselves. He looked edible tonight in a white shirt that hinted at the muscled flesh beneath. His honey-brown skin stood stark against the shirt under the interior lighting of the boat.

Loren had slutted me up good. My chin touched my boobs every time I lowered my head for a bite. But Tres kept his gaze trained on my face. He hung on my every word. The few I managed to get out during the second course, anyway.

We'd only gotten around to discussing the weather. He had little interest in movies and books, much preferring mathematics and engineering journals. We didn't share any friends in common who weren't Immortals. And it was hard to call Immortals *friends* since we couldn't spend too much time in one another's presence without getting sick. Neither of us had hobbies, only our life's work, which was in direct opposition to one another.

There wasn't much left for us to talk about except the one thing we had in common—ancient lands.

"Tell me about your new business venture?"

"Oh, no." Tres shook his head. "Work has always been a dangerous topic for us."

"Because you have no problem bulldozing your way through history?" I asked as I popped a poached strawberry into my mouth.

"I am not going there with you, Theta." Tres sliced his entree in perfectly straight, wholly equal pieces.

"What I don't understand is why not build in untouched places?"

"You mean like the oceans?" he asked, setting his steak knife at the side of his plate. "Cities are full of underutilized structures and lands that have cultural, social, or historical value. Those lands are the solutions to housing crises the world over where people can't afford the excessive costs of living. But instead, the privileged chain themselves to fences, color clever phrases on poster board, and say the people in need can't have a safe place to seek shelter because they, the privileged, are the ones protecting history. And you want me to put them in the oceans?"

His little speech left me tongue-tied. He waited a

moment for me to rebut. When I didn't, Tres charged forward.

"You seem to value the structures more than you do the people," he said. "I really don't get how I'm the bad guy in this story."

"You could compromise," I said. "Find sustainable ways to incorporate the old with the new."

"Reinforce the sites to add steel to the structures? Add indoor plumbing and communication lines? When I've done that, I've been accused of detracting from the original structures. I can't win for trying, so I prefer to simply win."

We sat in silence. Faced off. Utensils down. Arms crossed over our chests. Ready to strike, ready to defend. This seemed to be our natural stance when faced with each other across opposing lines.

I was the first to lower my defenses. "What did we used to talk about? When we were together before?"

Tres lowered his arms as well. His gaze turned heated. His eyes dipped to my breasts for the first time, or at least the first time that I'd caught him doing it.

"Oh." I gulped, resisting the urge to cover my

exposed cleavage. "So our relationship was mostly carnal?"

"No." He ran his finger around the rim of his wine glass. Then he smiled at me. Not at me, through me, as though he were seeing me through the sands of time. This smile was different than any I'd seen in the past few times we'd met on good terms. It was full of wonder and awe. I nearly missed what he said because I was so hypnotized by it.

"You were fascinated by architecture and engineering," he continued as he gazed at me. "You've always wanted to understand how things worked at a molecular level. Why a triangle instead of a square, you'd ask? You have an insatiable curiosity, and you never seemed able to fill it, which, I suppose, is why you forget things."

He looked down. I almost opened my mouth, but to say what? Apologize for forgetting him? I was constantly trying to regain my past, to regain anyone and everyone's past that had been lost.

"My focus is singular," Tres continued. "Like most of our kind. Bet and Yod want power and control. Delta likes to invent. Aleph wants to, let's say, find peace. But you? You want to know *everything.*"

A memory flashed through my mind of a time

when we were in Greece. I saw him building and directing crews as the boundaries of a city were marked off in the earth. In my mind, the city rose and fell, then rose and fell again. During one of these time-lapsed visions, I saw a wooden horse roll through the city.

"Tres? Did you build the city of Troy?"

He nodded, his chin rising a few millimeters higher.

"How many times did you build the city of Troy?"

His chin dipped, and he sighed.

To my recollection, there were nine cities stacked on top of the original city of Troy. That fact had been discovered in 1871 by Heinrich Schliemann. The way Schliemann had discovered it was using dynamite to dig through the layers, destroying some of his grand find. The idiot.

"Buildings aren't immortal," Tres said. "They're only meant to stand the test of human time, not ours. They crumble and decay while we remain untouched."

"So you just raze it like it never existed?"

"Seems to work for some people."

I jerked back. My steak knife clattered to the floorboards. I left it there.

Tres took another deep breath. "I'm sorry," he said. "For so long, the default between the two of us has been set to attack. The line between love and hate is truly thin with us. I don't want to fight with you. I'm trying to seduce you."

He paused and grinned at me. The grin was lopsided, just like our whole relationship. The edges were lumpy and wouldn't smooth out, no matter how hard we tried to press them down.

"This isn't easy for me, Nia. Fighting is the only pattern that *we* repeat."

It took me a moment to realize what he meant. What pattern he was pointing to. He'd mentioned that I had a pattern of going back to Zane. "This isn't about him," I denied.

"You always circle back around to him. It makes me wonder why I bother trying."

I didn't have words for Tres, but I was getting tired of being tried and convicted based on how I had behaved in the past—especially when I couldn't remember my actions. I pushed away from the table and went to the deck. I leaned on the railing, feeling the sea air whip around my face and cool me down.

The night was warm, but I shivered. Not because I was cold. Because I was uncertain. My shivering was short-lived as warmth grew at my back.

"That was a lie." Tres's voice was low as it rumbled along the back of my neck and down my spine. "I do know why I bother trying."

My hair was done up, thanks to Loren. Tres's lips brushed the place where my hairline ended and there was nothing but flesh. My breath caught at the heat that came from his lips.

"It's because you're a dish I tried long ago, and now I can't get the taste of you out of my mind. Others swear to me that they'll taste like you. But each time I take a sip, or a nibble, or a bite . . ."

His tongue sneaked out and licked at the side of my neck. So lightly I could've almost imagined it. The trail of fire he left behind let me know it was real.

"Every time I taste someone else, it's always a disappointment."

He tilted his head to the other side. This time, his teeth ran along my neckline. Without conscious thought, I tilted my head to allow him more access.

"I tell myself if I can just get one more taste of you, then I'll be sated." His lips touched my ear, whispering his confession. "But it's a damn lie."

He turned me in his arms. Or maybe I turned to meet him, I wasn't sure. The only thing that was solid was his lips against mine. He licked at the seam of my mouth. I sighed and opened for him. He nipped at my upper lip. His teeth took my bottom lip. And then he bit down.

The sting surprised me, and I jerked back. That was a mistake. He came after me. When his lips caught me this time, they attacked with everything he had.

I wrapped my arms around his neck to bring him closer. His big body pressed against mine, making me feel small and helpless. His hand went to my thigh. There wasn't much to the dress Loren had put me in. The span of his hand was longer than the fabric, so it was easy for him to sneak a finger beneath the hemline. When he did, he met with a surprise.

Tres pulled away and looked down at my exposed thigh. Instead of being put off, a salacious grin spread over his handsome face as he palmed my dagger.

"Habit." I shrugged.

"I remember," he said. His gaze locked on the steel against my skin. "And I still find it damn sexy."

I leaned in to recapture his lips, but he backed away. I frowned at him in confusion, but he only shook his head.

"I said no sex on the first date," he said.

"This isn't our first date."

"No, it's not." He grinned, but he still pulled away. "You had me on my knees by the time you let me into your bed that first time. I have every intention of returning the favor before I give you my virtue."

I didn't know whether to laugh or cry. In the end, I did neither. Tres returned to the table and picked up his knife and fork like a civilized man. It took me a moment before my legs would work, but I regained my seat. We ate our desserts in a silence punctuated with heated gazes as we each planned our next move.

CHAPTER TEN

My sleep was dreamless. There were no French artists with hooded eyes, or hands that created beauty, or arms that made me feel safe. But there was a blonde woman with light eyes who pulled me into a rude awakening.

"You think you're disappointed? Imagine how I felt to find you in your bed alone and not naked and wrapped around a billionaire."

I rolled over and pulled a pillow over my head. It was becoming a common occurrence in my life. But Loren, like always, was undaunted. She pounced on the bed, bouncing on her knees and then plopping onto her ass.

"The butler brought me heated towels today.

They were scented with lavender. Lavender, Nia. Please, I can't leave this place. Am I going to have to do everything myself? 'Cause I will take an L for the team and sleep with Tres."

"For your information, he's the one who didn't want to have sex on the first date."

The silence that ensued concerned me. Loren was never quiet. The few times she had been, it did not turn out well for me. I pulled the pillow off my head and flipped over.

Loren's face was screwed up in confusion. She opened her mouth and closed it a few times before words came out. "Is there a . . . problem? With his little submarine?"

"No, that's not it." I covered my face with my hands and shook my head. I'd felt his little submarine trying to rise to the surface when he'd kissed me on the deck. "He wants to have a relationship."

More silence. I pulled my hands from my face to see Loren's face twisted into a mockery of horror.

"Really?" She gagged. "But . . . but . . . he's a man."

"Yeah, he is. A good one, apparently."

She shook her head slowly from side to side. Her shoulders shrugged up to her ears. Her hands flopped over, palms up. "I have no idea how to proceed."

"I'm just as confused as you are. He wants to go on another date."

Her face lit up. "We're staying on the yacht?"

"No, we're going into Athens to find out about the Mysteries."

"Oh, yeah. That."

After packing up our belongings and dressing, Loren and I came up to the main deck. The city of Athens stretched out before us on Piraeus port. We were surrounded by ferries and cruise ships as the yacht maneuvered into a space to dock.

Tres stood at the helm of the boat. He wore a pair of dark trousers and a collared shirt with a few buttons open, exposing his chest. Standing in the light of the sun, he looked like a conquering warrior surveying his new lands.

He turned and saw me. A slow smile lit his face, and he crooked a finger. My brain revolted at being summoned, but my feet were already in motion.

I came to him and crossed my arms over my chest, staring up at him mulishly. "I told you, I don't take well to being bossed around."

He grinned. "Yes, you do."

He reached out, quick as a cat, and pulled me to

him. I was so startled that I gasped, my arms dropping from my chest and my lips parting. He had complete access to my body and my mouth. He leaned in and took advantage.

His tongue invaded and conquered, knocking down my walls before I could gather my defenses. I was so unguarded that memories shook loose in my head. I remembered a hard tug to my hair, a bite at the corner of my lip, a growl at the back of my ear, and a feeling of complete fullness.

In the memory, Tres was above me. His face was contorted in ecstasy. His eyes were lit with desire. His fingers dug into my hair and wrenched my neck back in ownership. And, God help me, I let him. It looked like I liked it. In my mind, I saw my eyes close as though I wanted more.

When he let me go in the present, I teetered. He'd taken his hands off me, but his body still pressed against mine. His lips still hovered above me.

"You two are headed to Eleusis?" He inclined his head toward Loren, who I was sure was giving me the thumbs-up sign behind his back.

"Yes," I managed through still-trembling lips.

"I'll be back in a few days. We'll have dinner."

"Okay," said a voice that sounded nothing like my own.

"When you find Demeter, tell her I said she still owes me for the Parthenon."

I nodded. Then his words registered. "You built the Parthenon?"

Tres winked at me as he took a step back. He opened the gate that would allow us to debark from the yacht. Then he turned back to me. "I'll call you." He looked over my shoulder. "Loren." He nodded.

Loren waved her fingers at him like the coquette she was. I knew she was serious about taking that L for the team if I didn't prove up to the task. I gave her a shove down the plank.

We took a taxi into the city and deposited our things in the Royal Olympic hotel, our base of stay. We planned to go to the city of Eleusis first thing in the morning. Granted, the invitation Baros had given us didn't give an address. Just a date and time. But history told us the initiations took place in Eleusis. The invitation said the initiation wouldn't happen for a couple of days, but we wanted to do some recon beforehand. Loren and I had already walked into one trap this year. Best to be prepared if we were heading into another.

The facilities inside the Royal Olympic hotel were old, but what it lacked in modern technology it made up for with its views. From my hotel room window, I could see the Temple of Zeus. Its ancient columns were close enough that I felt I could reach out and touch them. The Acropolis looked like a city in the sky.

"So, how do we find a Greek goddess?" Loren asked. "Saying 'Demeter, Demeter, Demeter' didn't work."

A knock sounded at the door. We stared at each other.

"Huh," Loren said. "Maybe it works when you're in Greece."

"Who is it?" I called out.

"Room service," a deep voice answered.

We stared at each other in silent debate, and then I went and opened the door.

Three men stood in the hallway. Not one of them had on hotel livery. Dark sunglasses covered their eyes. They had straight-lined cuts on their cheeks and hands, like they'd been sliced by a sword one too many times. Battle scars, definitely. But from what battle? No army used swords to fight, not anymore. The man in front shoved his way in. His strength caught me off guard.

"You two are coming with us," he said. And then

he did the stupidest thing a man could do. He grabbed my upper forearm.

"Dude." I shook my head, staring down at his massive paw on the sleeve of my shirt. "I have had enough of men trying to tell me what to do today."

When Tres had grabbed me and pulled me into him, it had turned me on. When anyone else tried to manhandle me? Nope.

The fist of my free hand cracked across the man's jaw. His upper lip went one way and his lower one went the other way. His teeth clattered from the impact. His head came to rest against his other shoulder. His hand let me go. But he didn't go down.

I had hit him hard enough to knock him out of the room, but he held his ground. His tongue came out, licking at the blood on his lower lip. His upper lip further separated from the bottom in a crooked smile. His head straightened as his gaze returned to me. His glasses were askew. His eyes were black, pupil-less pools.

A demon.

"Looks like you're going to struggle," he said. His voice sounded like rocks on a chalkboard. His coarse accent, along with the scars, reminded me of the gladiators of the Roman arenas. "I love it when they struggle."

The other two men stepped into the room, fanning out like warriors in an arena. They removed their sunglasses to reveal the same dark, empty gazes. Their massive bodies blocked the exit.

I took a step back and felt Loren at my side. The click of her cane and the slice of the blade that came out was loud. Though Loren was human, I knew better than to tell her to stay back. She'd faced down a ninja horde and held her own. She was a beast with that sword.

I grabbed the dagger strapped to my hip. "On three, we'll rush them. I'll take the two on the left. You take the one on the right."

"Got it."

"One, two, th—"

Loren rushed ahead. She lunged at her guy. He hopped out of her way—just barely—and reached in. She ducked, going low and getting in a slice at his thigh before swiveling behind him.

She looked over his massive shoulder at me. "Where are you? You said on three."

"No." I ducked a punch from one of my two guys. Then I pivoted and jabbed at the first guy, the one who'd grabbed me, slicing the fabric of his shirt. "You don't go *on* three. I say three and *then* we go."

"Then that's four." Loren slammed her guy in the

face with the blunt end of her sword. He was stunned for a second but shook his fat head and came at her again.

Before he reached her, another sword sliced between the two of them. Loren's opponent made a comical backpedaling motion with his feet while windmilling his arms until he came to a stop.

"Hello, Lolo." Leonidas Baros turned. His sword arced from the man's chest toward Loren, ending its point at the tip of her nose.

Loren looked from his sword's point and then to his face. A seductive smile spread across her features, but she didn't lower her sword. "Hey, Lenny."

While I continued to fight for my life against two massive men who seemed to enjoy my kicks and punches a little too much, Loren and Baros grinned like schoolkids at each other.

"Loren!" I called out.

"Huh? Oh, yeah." She stepped back and lifted her sword. It clanged loudly with Baros's. "Are these your men?"

"They are." With a flick of his wrist, Baros retracted his sword and brought it down against Loren's. But Loren went with the movement, warding off his strike with a circling motion that placed her sword on top of his.

"Very good." Baros's eyes twinkled as he admired the move.

"I learned from the best." Loren pulled her lower lip into her mouth. "You know, if you wanted to see me, you could've just called and asked me to come over."

"I didn't come for you," Baros said. "I came for your friend."

Said friend—that was me—now had three opponents she was facing off against while those two continued to bat eyelashes and rub their swords together.

"The boss wants to see Dr. Rivers," Baros said. "But I'm happy to see you again, Lolo."

"You are?" Loren asked.

"Yeah."

"Loren!" I called.

"What?" She turned to me, annoyed. "Oh, right." She turned back to Baros. "Can you call off your goons? They're roughing up my friend."

Baros whistled, and then growled, "Gladiators."

The men immediately dropped their arms. I didn't. I got in one last punch to the guy who'd grabbed me and one last kick to the third guy who'd joined the fray. Both men went to their knees.

"Whoa." Loren blew out a low breath. "That was kind of hot."

I knew she didn't mean my fighting skills. Mainly because she was still making goo-goo eyes at Baros. I marched up to the two of them, glaring at Loren, who shrugged with an insincere apology.

"You've been invited to a party," Baros said to me without giving me an ounce of his attention. His eyes were on Loren.

"Whose party?" I demanded.

"The Olympians."

CHAPTER ELEVEN

We stepped out of the room and into the elevator. The gladiators limped or cracked muscles and tendons that had met my fists or feet. I ran my fingers through my unmussed hair and straightened my blouse. When the elevator doors closed us in, Baros turned a key and pushed a button for the terrace instead of the ground floor.

"We're not going to Eleusis?" I asked.

"No," Baros answered.

"But that's historically where the rites have been held," I argued.

Baros turned and looked at me. His grin managed to be amused and condescending at the same time. "If I were trying to keep a secret, would I tell everyone, 'Hey, the answer is located here in this place?'"

I narrowed my eyes at the ass. Loren giggled at his mockery. I turned my glare on my traitorous friend.

"What?" she mouthed at me.

"It's a battle tactic to mislead the enemy," Baros said. "When the farce is known to all, you hide the truth in plain sight."

We were standing in an elevator going up and up and up. There wasn't much to see. I guessed I had to wait until the doors were open to see the plain sights he spoke about.

"So . . ." I decided to change the subject while we continued our ascent. "Baros, you had your soul taken?"

"I gave my soul freely," he said. "That's what separates me from a demon. A man, god, or Immortal who forcibly takes something that is not freely offered makes a slave out of a soul." He looked pointedly at me when he said the term *Immortal,* as though just the word burned his tongue. "You can tell a demon by the red rim around their eyes."

Now that he mentioned it, every demon I'd seen before had had the red rim around their eyes. They also weren't as vocal as Baros and his three gladiator goons. They'd been mindless fighting machines.

"When their eyes are red," Baros continued, "it means their soul was ripped from them."

"Without your soul, you still have free will?" I asked.

"I make my own choices. It's like a marriage. You promise to love, honor, and obey your spouse. You do everything with your spouse in mind, taking their welfare into account. But you can act independently. It's the same with a god. Death, in that case, just takes a lot longer."

"Wait, wait, wait. Hold up," Loren said. "Are you saying you're married?"

"I was," Baros replied.

Loren's eyes narrowed and her brow pinched. I was a bit surprised she was angry, considering she held no conviction to monogamy. But it was good to know there were lines, like marriage, that she didn't believe in crossing.

"My wife Gorgo died over two thousand years ago in Sparta." Baros's face looked solemn.

That appeased Loren, but it rallied my curiosity.

"Sparta?" I asked. "I thought you were Roman, a gladiator?"

Baros's lip curled in disgust. "I am a proud

Spartan. Son of King Anaxandridas. Trained since childhood in the art of combat of the battlefield and the political arena. I am not a sport fighter."

The three bruised gladiators in the back of the elevator bristled, but none spoke against him.

"Wait a minute," Loren said, her eyes widening in disbelief. "Leonidas? Spartan? OMG, you're the dude from *300*. Lena Headey, eat your heart out."

"That film was wholly inaccurate," Baros growled. "We didn't fight bare-chested; we wore armor. And that Persian pissant, Xerxes, wasn't nine feet tall. He was shorter than my son, and he never went to the front line of the battle."

"That's too bad," Loren said. "About the armor."

"Didn't you die in the battle of Thermopylae?" I asked.

"That was my intent," Baros said. "But the gods had more use of me."

"And so you gave them your soul?" Loren asked.

Baros nodded down at her.

"Why did you do it?" I asked. "Why did you give up your soul?"

He turned, taking his googly eyes off Loren for a moment to focus on me. "From what I understand of you, Dr. Rivers, you don't spend your immortality aiming to acquire power and dominion like others of your kind. You spend it chasing after the past. Why do you do so?"

"Because all stories deserve to be told," I answered automatically.

"My story wasn't finished. And so, when I got my invitation from the gods as I lay bleeding on the battlefield, I accepted. I proved myself worthy, and I was chosen."

"How did you prove—"

Before I could finish my question, the elevator came to a clanging stop and the doors opened. The gladiators stepped to the front and preceded us out, followed by Baros.

Loren tugged at my shirt. "Nia, did you hear that? I bagged a king."

"Good for you, sweetie."

"May I have that back now?" Baros stopped us as we came out of the elevator. His thick finger pointed at my chest.

I looked down and realized he indicated the ancient ring I wore on a chain around my neck. I gave it up grudgingly.

"By the way," I said. "Since you recovered the Nazi loot, did you find the Ninnion Tablet?"

"The what?" Baros asked.

"It's one of the artifacts that depicts the

Eleusinian Mysteries and the Rites of Demeter."

He chuckled. "I have not heard of such a thing. It must be some knickknack made by a human. There are many symbols and idols to the gods. We can't keep track of them all. This belonged to me before the earth swallowed it." He held the ring up between us. "A human dug it up and then put it in a museum. Then power-mad humans stole it before I could reclaim it. Through all that time, it never stopped being mine." He palmed the ring and turned on his heel.

"Was that his wedding ring?" Loren whispered as he walked in front of us.

I gave a fairly certain shake of my head. While the exchange of rings could be traced back to ancient Egypt and was a custom in ancient Greece, warriors didn't often have use of the custom. But most of my certainty came from the inscription on the ring. The word *justice* written in an ancient script that predated the Spartans didn't sound particularly romantic to me.

We walked up a narrow stairwell that opened out into the sunshine. I stepped out onto the terrace. For a moment, the sun blinded me as it reflected off the white temples that dotted the skyline.

This terrace was unreal. It looked on the outside

like a mini Parthenon with columns stretching high. If I thought the view from my room was amazing, the view from up high was spectacular.

I blinked as Baros beckoned me forward.

We were stopped at velvet ropes by a man with a sword and a shield. On the shield was a crest of wheat surrounding a scepter. I squinted at it as a memory tried to shake loose in my head.

"She can't enter." The guard pointed his sword at Loren. "She's not Chosen."

"She has accepted the invitation," Baros said. "She is an initiate."

The other man lowered the sword with reluctance. His eyes were trained on me in a look of disgust. Many of the Chosens' eyes were focused on me, their hands hovering over weapons at their sides. I supposed I'd been here before. But I had no idea what I'd done to piss them all off.

"Hey, Baros," I said as we crossed the ropes. "Other than Budapest, is this the first time we've met?"

"Yes," he said. "You are a favorite of the goddess Demeter. I am not her devoted."

"Oh," I said, keeping step with his wide stride while also making sure to steer clear of the pupil-less eyes that threw daggers at me from all sides.

"Did I piss her off, because a lot of these Chosen don't seem very welcoming."

"Most of the Chosen are Greeks. Greeks do not have a good history with the likes of you."

"The *likes* of me?"

"Persians." He spat the word.

"I'm not Persian."

"Immortals, then. Your brother Dio has never ceased in his hunger to occupy our homeland."

Dio was the word for the number two in Greek. "You mean Bet?"

"He is the one who guided Xerxes during my time. And then again led the sultans on their five-hundred-year occupation of my country. Even today, we are still at war over Crete."

Baros was right. Bet had a constant fixation on Greece and overpowering it. I had always assumed it was part of a larger plan, but now I wondered. What, who, exactly was he after?

I didn't have time to follow that line of thinking. As though he stepped out of thin air, Golden Rod from the orgy appeared and made his way toward us. Thankfully, he was clothed this time.

He wore an open shirt that showed off his toned chest. His golden hair framed his head like a crown, and his stride made me think he walked on air, like a sun god. I had to admit he made my mouth water. I swallowed quickly before he reached me, but he smirked like he knew the effect he had. Looking around, I realized it wasn't just me. Every pupil-less eye was on him. But he made a beeline straight for me.

"I knew you'd come find me." He reached for my hand and kissed it.

I felt tiny pinpricks of light zipping up my arm like sparkles during an American celebration of liberation. When his lips left my skin, it was replaced by a gush of his breath. The small puff of air blew at the embers left by the sparks. Still bending over my wrist, he tilted his head up and looked at me. His fiery eyes, along with the smoldering grin, set my skin aflame. I yanked my hand away.

"Leave her alone, Zuzu. She's here for me, not you."

Cradling my hand against my chest, I raised my gaze and saw a woman. She moved as if she floated. Her hair was the color of wheat. Her golden bright eyes were narrowed on me. She put her hands on her hips as she came to stand before me. Her lovely face did not look pleased.

"You bitch," she said.

"Pardon?" I asked, affronted.

"Zuzu said he saw you in Budapest. Psi said he saw you at sea. But I'm the last to know?"

"Um . . .?"

"I told you, Demi," Golden Rod, or Zuzu, said. "She doesn't remember."

"Nonsense," Demi countered. "Of course she remembers her best friend."

"Pardon?" Loren said, bristling at my side.

Demi ignored Loren and focused on me. "Don't you, darling? Tisa, it's me, Demeter."

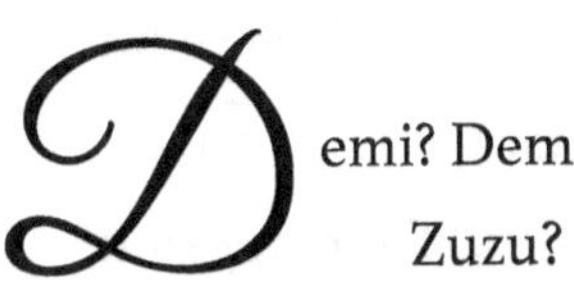emi? Demeter.

Zuzu? Zeus.

Psi? In the waters? The octopus that had winked at me. Had that been the Greek god of the oceans, Poseidon?

As if he heard me call his name, a tall drink of water approached us. His skin was deep brown. He had long, silky dreadlocks that floated around his shoulders as though a perpetual fan blew inches in front of his face. But the day was sunny and windless. His grin was cruel, promising wickedness. But it was his eyes that were most startling of all. They were as blue as the waves, and the color didn't stand still. It ebbed and flowed like the tide. When he spoke, his voice crashed into me like a tidal wave.

"Hello again, Tisa."

Poseidon didn't make a move to touch me, and I was thankful. Power radiated off him, as it did Demeter and Zeus. These were old beings. They didn't have an effect on me like my kind did. I didn't feel weak in their presence. I felt buoyed, lifted. But the feeling was new and scary for me, and I shied away from it.

Behind me, I felt something scorch my forearm. Zeus trailed a finger from my elbow to my palm. I snatched my hand away. He grinned unapologetically, like a misbehaving toddler who'd snuck his hand into the candy jar.

"She doesn't remember us, Psi," Demeter said, looking distressed.

"After all we shared . . ." Zeus tsked.

"Yeah?" Poseidon said to his brother. "You mean all the times she kicked your ass up to the sky?"

Zeus turned to glare at the other man, thunderbolts flashing in his eyes. "Thanks a lot, gutter-snipe."

Poseidon made a fist, and water splashed down on Zeus's head. Zeus glared and shook off the liquid like a dog would. The water flung from his body. He stepped forward without a drop on his person and not a golden hair out of place.

"I just did you a favor, baby brother." Poseidon grinned. "Now I won't have to rescue your balls from an Immortal's grip. Again."

Poseidon turned and winked at me. I offered him a smile of thanks. Then I turned my attention back to Demeter, who still studied me pensively.

"You told me you might forget," she said. "But I didn't believe you. You truly don't remember me?"

"Um . . . well . . ."

Before I could finish my hedging, she blinked and her face brightened. "This can actually work to my benefit. Any time we've squabbled, you've forgotten. Like any arguments over a certain pharaoh?"

"Who?"

"Exactly." Demeter grinned, spreading her hands wide. "It's like we're starting over. Demi and Tisa, the sequel."

"Um, hi." Loren stepped in front of us. "Loren Van Alst, current best friend, and the friend who knows better than to go after the same man as my bestie."

Loren turned to me for approval. I didn't mention that she'd made a pass at both my ex-boyfriend and the guy I was currently dating. I wasn't focused on my current friend. My gaze was fixed on my old friend, Demeter.

"Oh, look." Demeter folded her hands under her chin and grinned at Loren. "You've got a new pet. She's adorable."

I grabbed Loren's wrist before her hand could delve into her bag for her cane. "Behave," I whispered. "We're guests."

"Let her call me a pet again," Loren said through gritted teeth.

A brown-skinned woman with cropped hair and wearing a business suit stepped into the area from the elevator. She had a phone to her ear and was followed by a group of men and women with handhelds pressed to the sides of their faces. But it was clear that she was the epicenter of the group. Like Poseidon, her features were startling to behold.

"Tia," Demeter shouted. "Look who it is."

Tia came up to the group and stopped in front of me. Though she was a few inches shorter than I was, she managed to look down her nose at me. It took a second for recognition to dawn on her stern features.

"Oh. Tisa. Nice to see you again, I suppose. What's it been? About a thousand years or so?"

Her tone was clipped. Not in a mean-girl way. More in an inattentive, distracted way. Her gaze went from my face to her phone. It lingered far longer on her handheld than it did on me.

"Tia?" I said. "Do you mean . . . Are you the goddess Hestia?"

Tia tore her gaze away from her handheld and squinted her crystal blue eyes at me. "Of course I am. Have you lost your faculties in the last millennium? I hear that can happen to your kind. I'm quite certain your brother Dio is quite out of his mind. He's still causing trouble in the Aegean Sea, over some island or other this time."

I supposed she was talking about Turkey and Greece's continual dispute over Crete. I hadn't thought about it before, but it was very likely that Bet was behind it.

"Isn't that where you and Dio met, Demi?" Zeus asked. His eyes sparkled with mischief. "Perhaps that's why he wants the island? So he can destroy it? I love a good love story, don't you? Especially when it ends in bloodshed."

Zeus grinned at me. I looked from him to Demeter.

Demeter rolled her eyes and shrugged her shoulders. "Just a little lovers' spat. If he apologizes, I'll let him have it."

Hestia's phone beeped. She turned her back on us and faced the group of individuals behind her.

"We just landed the bid with the World Bank," she said. "Ari, can you take it on?"

A debonair-looking older man tapped on a handheld. His eyes were the dark ovals of a Chosen. "If Thag can lend me Hypatia to work on the numbers, then yes, my goddess, I can get right on the Euro crisis."

"Let's get to work then." Hestia went into motion, and the group fell into step. She turned and tossed over her shoulder, "Oh. Tisa. Good to see you. Welcome back. Et cetera."

I gazed after the group. Something looked vaguely familiar about the bunch.

"Hypatia?" Loren mused. "Wasn't she a famous Greek mathematician?"

She was. And those other two nicknames—Ari? Could that be Aristotle? And Thag—perhaps Pythagoras?

I turned to Demeter. "Aristotle? Pythagoras? Hypatia?"

Demeter nodded. "They're her Chosen. They run a number of think tanks the world over, solving political, economic, social, and technological problems."

I looked after them as they clustered around a table in the far corner of the terrace. Some of the world's greatest thinkers had, in fact, cheated death and were still solving the world's problems. I couldn't decide whether to be horrified or thrilled. My feet made to go after them to ask a million and one questions, but I was tugged in the opposite direction.

"I want to know about you, darling." Demeter looped her arm around my elbow and swooped me away from Loren. "What have you been doing these last thousand years? Come tell me everything. No, no, dearie, you stay here with the humans. There's a good girl."

Loren was too stunned to speak. I mouthed, *Chill,* to her. Luckily, Baros came up beside her. He looked amused by her ire as he tugged at her attention.

Demeter and I went off to the corner of the terrace. A man and woman stood near a fire under a mantelpiece with no chimney. The man's coloring was much like my own, but the hair on his face and chin was ginger. He clenched his fist, and the flame extinguished. Then he snapped his fingers, and the flame ignited. He was talking to a woman who sat beside him looking out at the monuments. It didn't look as though she responded to the man, and it didn't look as though he noticed.

"Desi, Hera, look who it is." Demeter gave me a shove forward.

The two looked up from their one-sided conversation.

"Tisa, my dear," the man, Desi, said. "How long has it been?"

"I'm not sure?"

From his casual playing with fire and the nickname, not to mention the devilish grin, this had to be Hades.

"I brought you a homecoming gift," he said.

He presented me with a ruby the size of my fist, and I nearly passed out. "I can't accept this." I almost added that it belonged in a museum, but I cradled it in my palm as it sparkled.

Hades shrugged. "It's no skin off my back, you know. There are millions more in the earth."

"You're a miner?" I asked.

He chuckled. "Why would you think that? Because mine is the realm of the underworld? I suppose next you'll assume I have dominion over all the souls cast down to Hell?"

"You don't?"

He cocked his head to the side. "I'm a film producer."

"That, and Desi has dominion over the minerals of the earth," Demeter said. "There are many precious jewels deep in the core, more than there are talented actors on the world's stage."

"But if I remember correctly," Hades said, "Tisa was never one to be impressed with shiny objects, unless it had some historical significance. This gem, I'm afraid, has no story. It is untouched by time."

"It's Nia now," I corrected.

"Nia . . ." Hades tested the name on his tongue. "I like it. I go by Desi now. Goes with the new image." He struck a pose in his dark jeans and Armani jacket.

"You're not what I expected," I said.

"Let me guess?" Desi grinned. "No horns."

I laughed.

"Come." Demeter tugged me to the table. "Sit. You must be hungry."

Zeus grabbed a seat next to me. "I think it's great we're starting with a clean slate."

Down at the end of the table, Hera, the only Olympian without a nickname, sat. She hadn't spoken a word to me but shot daggers down the table. She had blonde ringlets, like Zeus. But unlike Zeus, her skin was delicate, porcelain, near alabaster, as though she was the type to burn in the sunlight.

"That woman . . ." I asked.

Zeus poked his head up. "Oh, that's just my wife."

I cringed. "I forgot you married your sister."

He shrugged. "We were young. We'd just lost our parents. We took comfort in each other. It was a childish thing to do."

"That's still incestuous."

"Incest is a human concept. We're gods. We're not made like them. We don't share blood or genetics."

I looked around the table at this ragtag group. They were all beautiful, but none of them favored the other. Not Poseidon with his dark skin or Hestia with her bone-straight, black hair. Nor Hades with his ginger beard and Demeter with her wheat-colored hair. Nor Zeus with his golden good looks or Hera with her delicate ivory skin.

"Besides, we have an understanding, don't we, Hera?"

"If by understanding, you mean that you will screw a horse if you mistake its tail for a woman's long hair, then yes, I understand you completely, you ass." Hera turned her chair away from everyone.

Thunder crackled overhead as Zeus's jaw tensed.

"Speaking of family," Demeter said, "how is your brother?"

"My who?"

My heart arrested at the thought. We Immortals did not ever call one another siblings. Some of us did favor a bit. Vau and I had favored. Tres and Zane could be cousins.

"I haven't seen Bet since the Greco-Turkish War last century," Demeter said.

"Oh. Him. He's . . . good."

"In the Americas, last I heard?"

Demeter pulled her plate to the edge of the table. Her eyes were focused on cutting her meat, but I could see that her ears were perked up, awaiting any news of Bet. Unlike him with her, she appeared to have no aversion to saying his name. But there wasn't much I could tell her. Immortals didn't speak to one another like family. I may have seen Bet just a couple of days ago, but I didn't know how he was doing or feeling or what he thought any more than the next person. And that wasn't saying much.

Hestia joined the table, saving me from fumbling

through an answer. "Let's do the accounts before we eat, shall we?"

"Sorry, darling," Demeter said to me. "Just a bit of family business."

"Should I leave?" I didn't want to be parted from the food being placed before me. Or the company, if I were honest. I spent most of my time around humans, and there was something different about being around other Immortals. "I don't want to intrude."

"Of course you're not intruding," Demeter said. "You're one of us. Well, not a Titan god, but an Immortal."

I settled back in my chair. I cast a look at the other area, where the humans had clustered, and wondered how Loren was doing. No one was screaming for their lives, so I had to assume she was fine, especially if she had Leonidas Baros to occupy her short attention span.

"What's your take this month, Desi?"

"Twenty new initiates and two Chosen."

Demeter nodded. "Good haul."

"Fifty new initiates," Zeus said. "Ten Chosen."

"Zuzu, that's more Chosen than you're allotted."

"But I want them all." He pouted. "I got the MVPs of both the American Football League and the

World Cup. Not to mention five Olympic gold medalists."

"You'll need to make a choice." Demeter's tone was stern, like a mother's.

I leaned over to Poseidon, who sat on the other side of me. "You're choosing who will become demons?"

He raised an eyebrow.

"I mean Chosen."

Poseidon nodded.

"Why not take everyone who is willing?"

"If we took everyone, it would lessen the value of the offering. Scarcity makes people want it more."

"And you take their souls for . . .?"

"Sustenance."

I jerked back, horrified. "You eat people?"

He chuckled. "No."

I settled.

"Not their flesh. Only their souls. The consummation of a soul is powerful, but the charge it gives us lasts but an instant. Worship, given freely and continuously, is perpetual energy. People praising our names in words and deeds is what fuels us. That is why Desi is in Hollywood for much of the year, making movies about Greek gods. Tia keeps our names alive with the great thinkers of the world."

"What do you do?" I asked.

A sheepish smile crossed his handsome face. "I write books with our likeness for children and teens, to keep our names on the next generation's lips."

"Books? What books?"

Psi shrugged. "The most popular is the one where a child steals a thunderbolt from Zeus. Desi made that one into a film a couple of years ago, and it has done quite well."

I could only nod as I remembered seeing that series of books take over the bestselling walls of bookstores. And then I remembered little kids going wild at the opening weekend of the film.

Beside me, Poseidon shrugged again, as though it wasn't a big deal. "A god without a following of devotees simply ceases to exist."

"I don't have any worshipers or devotees," I said.

"You are not a god. You are something else."

"What? What am I?"

He smiled, but it was a sad one. "I don't know."

I got the feeling I'd asked him this before. I also got the feeling he was telling me the truth. He didn't know what I was any more than I did.

"How do you take a Chosen's soul?" I was too curious not to ask.

"You can come and see for yourself. The next rite happens in two nights."

I turned back to Demeter's accounting. She was now on Hera. "What is your take, Hera?" Demeter's tone was delicate, as though she were speaking to an invalid incapable of caring for herself.

"I have nothing to declare. I have no one."

There was silence around the table.

"That's nothing to worry about," Demeter soothed. "You are worshipped the world over. Women, mothers, wives lay wreaths at your temples daily, asking for your favor."

"They ask for my favor, but they do not choose to spend an eternity with me." Hera rolled her eyes, landing her gaze on me.

Well, not exactly on me. It was on the hand that had snaked around the back of my chair. I backed away from Zeus, whose fingers were entwined in the ends of my hair. Hera shot me a death glare before she turned away and picked up her silent seething once more.

Great. I'd made an enemy of a vengeful Greek goddess.

CHAPTER THIRTEEN

The fabric slipped down my body like butter on a warm croissant. Warm fall colors were my best complement. This dress wasn't quite red. It was hot and soft at the same time. Like fuchsia.

I eyed my phone, which sat in my purse pocket on the dressing room bench. There were no missed phone messages, no texts, no calls. I turned away from the silent device and faced my reflection.

"You look good enough to eat in that, darling." Demeter turned from her corner of the dressing room to take me in. Coming over, she twisted my body left and right. "You can go without the brassiere. Perpetually erect headlights are one of the more useful gifts of immortality, don't you think?"

I didn't know how to respond. She was touching me as though we'd been friends for years. And true, we had, but I couldn't remember. We were out at one of the most exclusive boutique shops in Athens for some girl time. Loren was back at the hotel. She'd pitched a fit when I told her where I was going, and worse, that she wasn't invited.

So far, the memories of Demeter were not coming back to me. The feeling of familiarity was present. From our easy interactions, it looked as though we had been good friends once. But she brushed off my attempts to delve deeper into our past connection, preferring to start fresh. Like Tres. And Zane. It left me feeling suspicious about what had gone down between us that she didn't care to resurface.

"Modern clothes are so confining, don't you think?" Demi slipped out of her dress. She wore no bra or panties. "I miss the days of peplos and togas. I nearly died the first time someone strapped me into a corset."

I laughed, remembering my first time in one of the confining medieval torture devices. I'd stayed out of civilized society as much as possible for most of the nineteenth century simply to avoid them.

A saleslady handed Demeter another dress, and

the goddess slipped it on. Often salespersons wouldn't let people try on their wares *au natural*. But this woman just beamed at Demeter as her lady bits made a direct impression in the garments.

"Oh, Your Worship, you look stunning," the saleswoman gushed.

"Yes, I do. Don't I?" Demeter turned left and right in the mirror, admiring herself.

The lady eyed Demeter with wonder and admiration. I felt a buzzing fill the room, like one would feel as churchgoers sang hymnals or rose their voices in prayer. I didn't frequent many churches, but I remembered that feeling. The power of it was unsettling to me.

"Oh, don't worry, darling," Demeter said. "That's just a side effect of a devoted."

"A devoted?"

Demeter nodded as she slipped the dress off and tossed it into a pile. "We'll take them all. Hers, too," she said, pointing at me.

I looked down at the price tag on the dress I wore. The scrap of fabric was more than an annual middle-class salary. I could afford it, but it was more extravagant than I usually spent. "I can't let you pay for this."

"Oh, I'm not paying for it, darling." Demi

laughed. Then she gasped, bringing a hand to her heart. "Don't tell me you're paying for things now?"

I pulled the dress over my head. Unlike my old bestie, I was wearing underwear. "We're not stealing anything."

"Of course not. I'm not a thief. I've never stolen anything in my life. Except a husband or two, but I gave them back after I was done."

The saleswoman came back and began folding the garments, then placed them in boxes and bags.

"These are gifts from our devoted." Demeter began putting her clothes back on. "A devoted is someone who praises the gods, but they aren't keen to go through initiation or the rites. The dressmaker is devoted to my sister Hera for her conception. Hera has many devotees but few Chosen. Most of Hera's worshipers are mothers, as she has a special knack for making babies. New mothers tend to want to keep the gift Hera gives them, even if it means they die within the century. Not everyone wants to live forever."

As I took in this tidbit of information, I followed Demeter out. Though we were both stronger than the two males helping us, they carried our packages outside to a waiting car.

"Is this what you do all day?" I asked, trying to get a little more information from her. We stood on the sidewalk, and I looked up at the cloudless sky. "Go shopping and get worshipped?"

"No, darling." She chuckled. "Not anymore. You inspired me to do more with my life. Now I sit on many boards to preserve culture, history, and identity. And I send out devotees and Chosen to recover much of Greece's lost antiquities."

"You sent Baros to get those artifacts from the Nazis?"

"Nasty group, them. Those and the Persians. The world would be better off without either of those lots."

I had no words. We could've been the same person. I spent my days uncovering and rescuing ancient artifacts, too. I'd never met a Nazi that I liked. But I didn't have a problem with Persians as a race, culture, or nation. Though there were a few who had gotten on my bad side over the centuries.

"But no," Demeter continued. "Baros did that on his own. He has a particular ax to grind against those who have done Greece ill."

I could imagine. The man had been king of this land once. He had watched it fall into the hands of many conquering and looting nations over the centuries.

Demeter looped her arm with mine. "Tell me what's going on in your love life. Are you still monogamous?"

She said the word like Loren would, and I chuckled. But then I realized who she was talking about. Tres had mentioned she had a preference in my lovers.

"Zane and I aren't . . . we . . ." Why couldn't I bring myself to say it?

"Really?" Demeter didn't seem to need a completion to the sentence. "He was utterly devoted to you. What did he do?"

"How are you so sure it was his fault?"

She frowned at the question, her brows screwed in incomprehension. It appeared she didn't even think for a second that I could have done something wrong. I could see why I liked her in the past. She was growing on me here in the present.

"I'm dating someone new now," I said. "Well, he's a past paramour."

"Don't tell me? Is it the Arrogant Architect?"

I laughed. First, it was the Broody Billionaire, and now, it was the Arrogant Architect. "What's wrong with Tres?"

"Is that what he's calling himself these days? Nothing's wrong with him, darling. He's a perfect specimen of man. Just too bossy for my tastes. The type who thinks he knows it all. Tia told him the columns of the Parthenon needed to be adjusted by two inches or it would collapse in two millennia. She was right. But dally with him again if it pleases you."

If she was being tight-lipped about our past, I wondered if she might loosen them about my past with Tres. "Do you remember when he and I were together? Before?"

"Just the end of it, I think. About a thousand years ago or so? You and I only saw each other briefly. We had a bit of a falling out back then."

"We did? Why?"

"It was so long ago." Demeter shrugged, not meeting my eye. "I can't quite remember."

I didn't believe her, but I was used to other Immortals not telling me the whole truth. So I asked her another question I thought she would answer. "Do you remember why Tres and I broke up?"

She did meet my gaze then. "Because you went back to Zayin."

Thunder crackled overhead in the clear blue sky. People dashed under awnings to escape the downpour that only seemed to hover around them. Where Demeter and I stood was dry, not a drop fell.

"Really, Zuzu?" Demeter huffed. "Maybe if you stopped acting like a randy little boy, she would actually take the time to talk to you. Instead, you resort to trying to get her wet."

"That's the plan," came a deep masculine voice.

I turned and saw Zeus sitting at a café beneath an umbrella.

"Nia, if you just sleep with him once, he'll probably leave you alone." Demi snorted. "He has a shorter attention span than a gnat once he's gotten what he wants."

"You can control the weather?" I asked, looking out at the rainstorm.

"Ha," he said. "Is that all it takes to impress you?"

I turned my attention from the shower and focused on him. The man was breathtaking to behold, but his antics were entirely off-putting. "Why do you act like such a child?"

"I've never been a child," he said. "I came into this world a fully-formed adult. I suppose that's why."

"You remember your birth?"

Zeus's face changed. It turned grave. The

childishness fell from his features, and he looked like a very old man. "Yes," he said simply.

Beside him, I felt Demeter affect the same carefully blank look. A breeze tousled her hair and made her look like she was floating. It jogged a memory.

"You were in my dream," I said.

"You dreamed of me, darling?" She smiled.

"I was dreaming about a memory, and then you stepped into it. You seemed distressed. You told me to wake up and remember."

"That doesn't seem like something I'd say," she said. "I'd be more likely to urge you to sleep it off and forget."

"Is that your power? Can you dream walk?"

"Of course not."

Once again, her face changed. Instead of carefully blank, it was false amusement. Her laughter was forced.

"Wouldn't that be an awesome power?" she asked. "I'd wreak havoc on the world. You must have been remembering me, darling. I was a very big part of your life once."

I chanced a look at Zeus. For once, he kept his eyes off me and on the ground. This type of Immortal behavior I knew. They were hiding something. They wouldn't come out with it, not directly. Luckily, I knew how to do this dance. I had to twirl and spin around the issue until I tripped them up.

"When we knew each other before," I said, "was that in Egypt?"

"We spent some time together in Egypt, yes." Demeter's tone was careful.

"When my temple was being built?"

"Your temple?" She rose an eyebrow.

"Yes, the Temple of Isis at Philae."

"Oh no, no, darling." Demeter shook her head. The amusement this time was genuine. "That's my temple. I was known as Isis in Egypt before we came here to Greece. Oh, darling Tisa, your brain is well and truly addled, isn't it?"

I jerked back. She wasn't dancing around the issue at all. She'd gone and put her foot in her mouth. But she didn't seem to notice. These gods had once been worshipped in Egypt. So why had they left and come to Greece?

"We had many followers when we lived in Egypt," Zeus said. "But they soon began worshiping the Christian god, and our following decreased so substantially that we were near to fading, like our parents."

"We don't talk about them." Demeter's voice was a harsh admonishment to her brother.

"Because they tried to eat you?" I asked.

The two didn't favor in looks. But once again, they shared the same expression. Their jaws clenched, both looked wholly uncomfortable at the direction of the conversation.

"They did eat us," Demeter confirmed. "But Zuzu saved us."

I wanted to ask how, but Zeus had his arms crossed over his chest. It was a universal sign for *I don't want to discuss it*. I could imagine. Being eaten had to be horrible. I'd nearly been consumed myself. I decided to back off. For now.

"Don't hold that against them," Demeter said. "They were desperate. We were the only ones who still worshipped them."

"Until they tried to steal our essence." Zeus's handsome face had darkened like the sky above him.

"Calm down, Zuzu. You're ruining a perfectly good day." Demeter turned back to me. "A god never truly dies. We are made of existence, that spark of life. Humans gift us with their spark with their worship and their souls. Their continued devotion fuels us, and we reward them with riches, fame, beauty, children, long life. It's a perfect symbiotic relationship. Don't you see?"

I didn't see, but I was curious to find out, so I nodded my head.

Demeter smiled at me and looped her arm through mine again. "Oh, it's so good to have you back, Tisa. There's so much to catch up on."

CHAPTER FOURTEEN

"Where are we headed now?" I watched the scenery of Athens zip by out the window of the car. I was half surprised we weren't flying on a cloud to wherever we were going, or traveling by Pegasus. Then I wondered if there were such creatures in the world. But when I turned to inquire with Demeter, her gaze was sorrowful.

"There's some family business I need to take care of," she said. "Do you mind, darling?"

We'd left Zeus behind. Or rather, he'd left us after he'd seen a pair of buxom twins walking down the street. I'd felt a moment's irritation that his eye had been so easily turned, but it was just my pride smarting. I had no intention of letting that man's overused ego anywhere near my pride. Besides, I was having an enjoyable time with his sister.

"Sure," I said. "As long as we don't have to knock off someone."

Demeter didn't laugh. Loren would've laughed. When I turned to Demeter again, she looked grave.

"We're not knocking someone off, are we?" I asked.

"It's a farewell party. One of the Chosen has asked for the return of his soul."

"They can do that?"

"Well, of course they can, darling. We're not slaveholders. An undevoted soul does us no good. If we hold them against their will, they could turn into demons."

Demeter grimaced as though the word *demon* left a foul taste in her mouth.

"This individual has served us well for over two millennia. I, for one, will be sad to see him go. I believe you may have met him. Yes, in fact, I know you did. You brought him to us."

"Who?" I asked.

"I'll let it be a surprise. You'll be my present to him. There at his rebirth, and there again for his final death. Poetic, don't you think?"

I didn't know what to think. "You're throwing him a farewell party?"

"A farewell party sounds better than a wake, darling. But I prefer to think of it as a retirement. Nothing ever truly dies. Once his soul is returned to his body, he will be parted from us and returned to the source of all life. One day, his essence will be recycled. A new spark will bring him back to life again."

That was what happened to humans. I'd witnessed reincarnated souls many a time during my long life. I'd looked into the eyes of unfamiliar faces and seen old souls. *Déjà vu* was more than a feeling—it was a memory from the past.

The car pulled to a stop. Out the window, I saw Hestia march down the steps in heels and a business suit, a phone pressed to her ear. She got in the car and off the phone.

"How are tricks, Tia?" I asked.

When I got a befuddled frown in response, I tried again.

"Demi said you run think tanks all over the world?"

Hestia nodded. "I loan out my thinkers to Fortune 500 corporations, governments, and nonprofits. I give my Chosen the money, and I get their praise. Wonderful exchange. By the way, Demi, Psi said he's biking over."

"For gods' sake, we're carpooling like he asked." Demi shook her head. "My brother, the environmentalist. He won't save the world huffing uphill."

"I'm a little shocked that you all have jobs," I said. "I wonder, what does Hera do?"

They looked at me in silence for a moment.

"Hera has done a lot of work in the area of human fertility." Demeter seemed to choose her words carefully.

That made sense. Hera was the goddess of fertility and mothers. "*Has* done? She doesn't do it anymore?"

"She's been a bit restless and aimless the past few hundred years," Demeter said.

"She's trying to find herself." Hestia's voice had the same monotone, but I sensed there was a bit of mockery in her words.

"She doesn't really need to do much," Demi continued. "Her favor is sought by millions of women daily. She'll be sustained for all time so long as babies need to be born and people wish to be married."

To me, Hera hadn't looked like she was pleased

with her lot in life. The way Demeter spoke of her sister was as though she were trying to overcompensate for the middle child whose career never took off. Hestia and her brothers didn't seem to care about Hera's sullenness the other day up on the terrace. Zeus definitely paid his sister-wife little attention.

I decided to leave that matter alone and inquire about something else that had been on my mind. "Are there only the six of you? Where are the other gods of Olympus? Athena, Apollo, Persephone. Your children."

Hestia looked up from her phone, her thumb paused over the screen. Demeter's smile wobbled.

"Those are myths, darling," Demeter finally said. "Stories made up by humans as they tried to explain away the things they could not understand."

"And it was a way for them to keep the many pagan gods they used to worship," Hestia muttered, her head bent back over her phone.

"We're gods, darling," Demeter said. "We're not like them. We can't have children with humans."

"What about with each other?" I asked. "You had parents."

And there was that tension again. Hestia's fingers froze over her phone. Demeter's jaw tensed as it had done on the curb with Zeus when I'd asked about her parents.

"A discussion of my parents' sex life." Hestia shuddered. "There goes my appetite."

"You've forgotten, Nia," Demeter said. "It doesn't work that way with us."

I couldn't push the issue any further. The car came to a stop. When the door opened, we were at one of the most exclusive restaurants in Athens.

Inside, we were ushered to a private room where many had already assembled. Hera sat talking with an old man and a few dark-eyed Chosen. Poseidon leaned against a wall in board shorts and a tank top. Next to him, Hades stood looking every bit the movie producer in a tailored suit and sunshades.

Unlike the others gathered, who were all impeccably dressed, the white-haired man in the seat of honor was barefoot. His feet were ashen and his toenails ragged. His clothes were disheveled as though he'd thrown them in the wash only just before coming to the party. His hair was a wild array of white wisps. His nose was bulbous and crooked. His nostrils flared as though he was taking the room in by both sight and smell. His large eyes were as wide as his face, which made his opaque, pupil-less gaze even more arresting.

His pale gaze, unlike the darkness of the Chosen I'd seen before, reminded me of the Greek busts seen throughout the world in museums. I wondered what made his gaze white instead of black? Perhaps it was his age? Demeter had said he was over two thousand years old.

The mood in the room was as somber as it would be in a funeral hall. Only the man whose life was soon ending seemed happy. He stood when the other two Olympians entered the room.

Demeter reached her hands out to him, and he grasped them with his own. "Are you sure there's nothing we can say or do to change your mind, Socrates?"

I stopped in my tracks. I stared at the twenty-five-thousand-year-old man as he bowed over Demeter's hands.

"The world has borne my radical ideas long enough," Socrates said.

He turned to me and smiled. "Tisa?" he asked. "Is that you?"

It didn't feel like he was confirming my name. He was Socrates, after all. The great questioner. I felt like I was being tested, and I didn't know the answer. These past two months without Zane, I had been searching for my identity. Was I Tisa? Was I Theta? Maybe I was Nova?

"I go by Nia now."

Socrates embraced my hands, his large, gnarled fingers encasing my own. I was surprised at his strength. "It has been too long. I would've asked to die sooner if I'd known it would bring you back into my presence."

I forced a smile. I had to since the memories of this great man wouldn't come to my mind. "What have you been doing all these years?"

"The same thing I did every day as a mortal man—asking questions."

"Will you tell me what you've learned?"

"The same lessons as when I was a boy." He grinned secretively. "I know that I am intelligent because I know that I know nothing."

"That sounds . . . disappointing."

Socrates laughed. "No, my dear, it's freeing. I've been holding on for all this time, hoping that some great mystery would be revealed to me, all to find out that I knew it all along. I knew it the moment I was born."

"You knew what?"

He smiled. It was a wizened smile, filled with joy, sorrow, and certainty. "That I am ignorant."

"I know you're about to die and all, and this may sound callous, but that's stupid."

"Precisely." He grinned. "And you are unchanged. I can tell that you're still seeking to know everything. But it still comes to pass that the more you learn, the less you know. Quite literally with you. I can see that you don't remember me."

I knew of him. But he was right. I couldn't remember any personal interactions with either him or these gods. Once again, I had written down everything but the good stuff about history.

"I once told you that education is the kindling of a flame and not the filling of a vessel," Socrates said. "That burning desire you have will never sate you, Nia. It will never fill you. It can only burn away the flesh of yesterday and make way for a new you that comes with every tomorrow."

"Can I ask you a question?"

"That's how I died the first time." He winked at me. "I asked too many questions. But worse, I made the youth think."

I remembered the trial of Socrates. He'd been accused of corrupting youth, but that wasn't the whole story. "History says you committed suicide?"

He chuckled. "Being impervious to death

yourself, have you ever had to fake your demise to get out of a tricky situation?"

I had. "Why now? Why are you choosing to end your life in this time?"

"I was fortunate to choose my rebirth, and now I am fortunate to choose my death. I have examined all of life. There is nothing left to say or think on. Information is so readily at hand and opinions are so widely available that no one needs to or cares to think for themselves any longer. It feels less and less like a democracy and more like a hive mind. That's what happens when a power vacuum comes into existence. It's the reason I died the first time."

In Ancient Greece, during Socrates's time, the great ruler Pericles died of plague after a military campaign gone wrong. So many jockeyed for power in his wake. One of the tools they used to snatch power from one another was pointing to scapegoats such as Socrates.

"My life's work was to foster the knowledge of the next generation. But I no longer feel needed in a place that thrives on recycling the old and not generating new ideas."

"So you're giving up?"

He gazed at me. Though his eyes were opaque,

they weren't expressionless. He looked tired but determined.

"No," he said. "I am looking for a new challenge. The flesh is not built for eternity. I have been seventy for hundreds of years. My bones have creaked, my heart has been sluggish. Only my mind has been bright. But with the pace of today's world, I've grown tired. I can't keep up with the speed of change and the lack of attention. These handheld devices make me shudder."

"Me too."

"I've left my mark. Now my soul is weary and I'd like to rest."

"There's a difference between growing up and growing old."

He smiled. "Yes. Exactly."

CHAPTER FIFTEEN

*L*oren's eyes widened at the designer shopping bags I brought into the hotel room later that evening.

"So, not only did I get relegated to the kiddie table last night, but I got left out of mall shopping—no. Strike that. High-end boutique shopping."

Her fingers traced the embossed letters on the face of the box that displayed the name of the exclusive shop I'd spent my morning at. I pulled out another with the same fancy lettering and presented it to her. She snatched it and pulled out a dress in her size. Her mouth fell open in a soundless gasp and then she let out a high-pitched squeal of delight when she held up her present.

"This softens the blow," she said. "But you are

not forgiven. I should send you back to that store to think about what you've done while you get me a pair of shoes to match."

"I didn't buy it. Demeter did."

Loren scrunched her nose, but she didn't put down the dress.

"And she didn't buy it," I continued. "It was gifted to her by one of her devoted."

"Now I don't know if I should cheer her for getting free stuff or hate her for being worshipped. You do know that the Olympian gods killed their parents, if mythology is to be trusted?"

"The mythology said it was in self-defense. Because their dad ate them up."

Loren toyed with the designer label sewn into the collar of her dress. "Do you think that really happened?"

"Apparently, it did. But they don't like to talk about their parents." Demeter and Zeus's stoic faces flashed before my eyes, as did Hestia's thumb hovering over her handheld. "They get touchy every time you make a reference to them."

"Well, I would too if my mom and dad served me up with a side of potatoes. Oh my God." Loren rubbed her cheek against the hem of the dress. "Is this real cashmere?"

"But I don't think they're dead."

"You mean Cronus and Rhea, the Titans?" Loren spoke to me, but her attention was still on the dress.

"Demi said gods never truly die."

That got her attention. She dropped the dress on the bed and shoved her fists into her hips. "Demi?"

"Hey, I had a life before you," I said in my defense. "Just like you had a life before me, *Lolo*."

Loren rolled her eyes as I tossed Baros's pet name at her. "Nia's already too short for a nickname."

"I'm not trying to replace you."

"Of course not, at least not for another eighty years at best. Unless . . ."

I turned to face her, but she only gave me her back. "Loren? Are you thinking about accepting the Olympians' invitation to become a Chosen?"

She shrugged without turning around. I rounded on her, but she didn't meet my eyes. While Loren looked down, I took a moment to consider what I wanted her answer to be.

The last best friend I had who wasn't human, Vau, had died a terrible death. I'd been too late to save her. The other best friend who wasn't human, Demeter, was hiding something from me. Loren hadn't always been exactly forthcoming with me, but

I knew she'd be there if something terrible were about to happen to me. I'd be there for her, too.

"Do you want to be initiated?" I asked. "Then you could be a perpetual annoyance instead of a temporary one."

Loren shrugged. The nonchalance of the move caused a pang in my chest, like something inside me was preparing to shrink a few sizes. I decided to try a different tactic.

"You could hang out with Baros more," I said.

"You know I don't believe in monogamy. But at the same time, I have jealous tendencies. I don't like other people touching my stuff." She gave the bags of gifts from Demeter a cold stare.

Impulsively, I wrapped my arms around her and gave her a bear hug. "I am your stuff, RenRen."

She gasped. "Did you just nickname me after a cartoon dog?"

I snorted, hopping back before she could attack. When I plopped down on the hotel room bed, she came to sit beside me.

"I don't know what I want to do with my life," she said.

Her gaze went unfocused for a moment, and I held still with her in the silent indecision, not trying to exert my will upon her. It was her soul at play, her life, not mine. Like the gods who could grant her everlasting life, I had to respect her decision.

After a while, Loren's gaze focused. It sharpened on the top of the box that her dress had come in. "I still think something's not quite right with these gods."

"Yeah, me too. They are a strange lot, but what family isn't? They do actual good for the world. Organized good. I feel like my kind has brought nothing but strife."

Bet and Yod caused countless wars in bids for power. Tres built and demolished. Zane made beautiful things, but then he committed murder without an ounce of remorse. And that was just four of the ten who remained.

"I think we need to continue our initial mission," Loren said.

"I agree. The Ninnion Tablet may be lost, but there should still be some trace of the Mysteries around here."

"Let's head out to Eleusis tomorrow. Maybe we'll find something there about the rites that the Olympians aren't telling us."

"All right," I agreed.

"And if we find any incriminating evidence on your new BFF, that will just be a boon."

"Yeah, I guess." When I turned, Loren was glaring at me with a look of accusatory disappointment. "What?"

"You're supposed to say, 'I'm your BFF.'"

"Loren, you're my BFF," I said in a stilted voice. Then I ducked before she could toss a pillow at me.

The drive to Eleusis was short and lovely. Once there, we were met with more ruins than what was found at the Acropolis. It looked as though a giant had knocked down the monuments and temples at the site and then laid down in the ground. A huge mound rose in the midst of the debris. The white columns lay in fields of green grass and yellow flowers. Tourists walked the ruins freely. There were no engineers around trying to piece the place back together. It was eerily silent except for the clicks of cameras.

I didn't think I'd been here before, but something about this place felt familiar. I felt I just needed to look harder and I'd see it. But there wasn't much to see.

We stood in the remains of the Telesterion. It was once a large, rectangular hall where ancient rites and religious celebrations had been held. Now it was a pile of rocks in the center of a ruin. I saw circular disks protruding from the ground, which were likely once columns. It would've been a sight two thousand years ago, before it was destroyed by the Persians in the Battle of Thermopylae.

Today, there were a few men and women laying wreaths and flowers at the base of the temple. Upon closer inspection, it looked as though they were laying wheat.

"What are they doing?" Loren asked.

I racked my brain for an answer I knew was there, but someone else beat me to it.

"They are making an offering to the goddess Demeter," said a male voice.

We looked over to see a man walking toward us. He was dressed in a vest with the Greek word for *docent* embroidered over the breast pocket.

"This served as the initiation hall and temple for the Eleusinian Mysteries." The docent's English was thickly accented. In his hands, he held poorly copied brochures on cheap copy paper. The script indicated he was an expert on the Cult of Demeter.

"If you were a devotee of the goddess Demeter and her daughter Persephone, you would enter the Telesterion and be shown the sacred relics of Demeter by the priestesses. Through a fire, they would reveal their visions of the holy night to you. If you were found worthy, you would be initiated into the next life."

"What next life?" I asked.

"I can't tell you." He grinned. "I'm sworn to secrecy on pain of death. But the rites will be held here in three nights' time for the truly devoted."

He held up an invitation. It was not like the one Loren and I had been given by Baros in Budapest. But I had seen it before. It was the one held by the girl who was denied entrance into Zeus's orgy party. It had the same image of woven wheat, but this time it was surrounded by black and white peacock feathers.

"The mystery cult is very particular about who they let in," the docent was saying. "But I could get you ladies an invitation . . . for a price."

Before I could say anything, Loren grabbed the man's collar and twisted. "I can offer you money or I can offer you pain, but one way or another, you'll tell us exactly what these rituals are."

The man squealed, but then he spilled. "It's just a bunch of college kids and stoners. There were invitations sent out online for a Spring Break party. They'll dress in the old style, read the story of Demeter and Persephone, take some hallucinogens, and probably pass out in the fields. It's all in good fun. No harm done."

We waited for him to say more, waited for the great conspiracy, waited for the bad guys to jump out from behind the ruined temple and attack. But no one came. The docent said no more words. He only whimpered.

"That's it?" Loren asked, letting him go. She seemed angrier at the con than she was at the man.

"Of course," he said. "It's not real. The real ritual used to be held on this very night, the solstice. But most people come down a few nights from now, when the universities let out. We may get a few dozen college kids or so. Hardly anyone comes anymore."

"But they used to come?" I asked. "In the past?"

"Sure," he said. "About a hundred years ago when the Ninnion Tablet was here. But since it was lost, people have lost interest."

"Are there any depictions of the tablet here in the temple?" I asked.

He shook his head. "I've never seen any. But I heard that what was on the tablet was just the image of people making an offering of wheat to the goddess, Demeter. You do know there's no such thing as gods, right?"

We only stared at him.

"I'll take that cash now," he said, dusting himself off.

Loren cocked her fist back. Before she could unload, the man cowered and then hurried away.

I turned to the crumbling structure. There had to be something more. I could feel power in this place. The temples had been decimated by invaders during the Persian invasion. It had been rebuilt and destroyed again during the Peloponnesian War. There were layers beneath the ground. Perhaps we could find something hidden beneath?

But looking around the town, it was clear its glory days were gone. This might be the place where humans had held festivals in praise of the goddess Demeter in the past. But with her expensive tastes and luxurious lifestyle, I doubted Demi spent any time or thought on this place any longer. If there was something going on, it wasn't happening here.

"Looks like there's no smoking gun here." Loren huffed. "No sacrificial altar. No burial mounds of Cronus and Rhea."

At the mention of those two names, the wind kicked up on the cloudless sunny day. I felt prickles on my neck. "Do you feel that?"

"Feel what?" Loren asked, seemingly unaware of any change in the atmosphere.

A buzzing sound filled the quiet. I felt it shaking my leg. I reached into my pocket and pulled out my phone. On the face was a text message from Tres.

Back in town tomorrow. Can we do lunch?

I stared at the words on the phone. Unlike in the past, when I used to get text messages from Zane, Tres's message had come through without delay. And none of the words were scrambled by the auto-cucumber. I could read his message loud and clear.

So, how would I respond?

A sleek luxury car pulled up at the hotel that night. I was expecting Demeter, but I saw masculine legs stretched out in the interior. I rolled my eyes, thinking I'd have to spend the drive fending off the advances of a golden god on the way to Eleusis. Luckily, I didn't think Zeus would try to maul me with Loren in the car.

But then, Poseidon's dark head leaned out of the car and reached out a hand. He first guided Loren into the car and then reached back for me.

"I thought you were against air pollution from cars?" I said.

"It's a hybrid," he said. "Besides, it would be bad form to take a lady out for the evening and expect her to ride a bike or walk."

His lips curved up to his cheek, much like the silky locks that rested on his shoulders that begged to be stroked by a lover's hand. His smile was not set to seduction. He wasn't hitting on me, and I couldn't decide if I was disappointed by that or not. Poseidon oozed sexuality, but unlike his golden-haired brother, he didn't wield it like a weapon. But Psi and I knew that if that lazy grin ever turned all the way up and he flashed those shark-bright teeth, neither I nor any woman would be able to keep hold of her panties.

"Will you tell us more about these Mysteries?" Loren asked. "Will there be any bloodletting? Is it sexual?"

"No." Poseidon's grin was indulgent. "No blood or sex. There's a ceremonial exchange of vows, much like a bride and groom, or a nun, or a priest. And then there's a reception."

"That's it?" Loren sounded disappointed.

"I'm sure Leonidas will be happy to engage in the other activities you mentioned." Poseidon winked.

No sooner had the car started and we pulled into traffic than we were stopping.

"Where are we?" I asked. "This can't be Eleusis."

"No," Poseidon said. "Why would you think we were going there?"

We stepped out of the car, and I saw the golden illumination of the Parthenon at night. The artificial lights glowed off the fifteen thousand pieces of marble. After two millennia of succumbing to the whims of man and the ravages of nature, the building was crumbling. The columns looked as though they'd been clawed out by a minotaur or a kraken. But I knew that the central portion of the building had been blown out during the Great Turkish War of 1683 when the Turks stored gunpowder in the sacred place. Three of the sanctuary's four walls had been badly damaged and many of the sculptures from the frieze fell, as did the roof.

Where the sculpture of Athena once stood, a crane now occupied the space. Men and women surrounded the crumbling marble, trying to save it. Pristine pieces of freshly cut marble mixed in with the cracked and decayed pieces like a jigsaw puzzle.

The restorers continued to work under the moonlight, dedicated to saving this piece of their culture. They used what looked like dental tools to strip the botched work of restorers of the past. They flushed out the corrosive materials used years ago on a botched rescue attempt with the cleansing tool dentists used to irrigate the jowls, and followed that with actual toothbrushes to brush away the grime.

Poseidon, Loren, and I walked up the steps that led to the ancient temple. There were metal handlebars and scaffolding mixed in with the ruins. There were now steel railings affixed to the pathway. A million people visited this attraction each year.

One of the workers turned to us, as though to halt our progress. Poseidon raised his hand. The official's eyes glazed over. He blinked and looked through us, then shook himself and turned back to work.

"What did you do to him?" I asked.

"Hid us from view," Poseidon answered.

"You can control the minds of humans without their consent?"

"It was only a gentle nudge and it was against his will, so it won't last long."

We continued through the Parthenon and went into the restricted area of the columns.

"Why don't you just compel everyone to worship you?" I asked.

"It's a matter of quality," Poseidon said. "You can force someone to give you attention, but you can't force them to love you. That must come freely. And when it does, you know the difference."

He looked at me knowingly. Then he cocked his head to the side. Those clear eyes regarded me with interest.

"How is Setuk these days?" he asked.

"We're not together anymore. I'm . . ." I'd set my mouth to say I was with Tres, but I didn't. I wasn't exactly with him. More circling around him. Maybe.

"I saw you with Horus." Poseidon grinned.

Oh, yeah. He'd been in the waters while we were on Tres's boat. Poseidon offered no judgment on my choices in partners, which made me want to know his thoughts on my love life. I wondered what our relationship had been like in the past? There were secrets behind his still-water gaze. Though something told me they had nothing to do with me.

Before I could ask, he reached out and turned a latch on a doorway. A passageway opened. We went in and down.

"Is this another layer of the Parthenon?" I asked.

"This is the temple that was built here before the current building above us. It was destroyed by the Persian Invasion of 480 BCE. By your brother, Osiris."

I knew he meant Bet. I hadn't heard anyone call him that Egyptian name in thousands of years since he'd left Egypt for Asia.

"And then your brother Horus built the current temple," Poseidon continued. "It was your brother Setuk that erected the statue of Athena, or who people believed to be Athena."

"They're not my brothers," I insisted in a huff. The mere thought of shared blood between us made me shudder.

Poseidon only grinned at me as though it was a joke we'd shared in the past. Only I'd forgotten the punchline and still didn't see the humor today.

We entered a room full of individuals dressed in robes. I looked to Loren. Both she and I were in slacks and blouses, completely underdressed.

Baros approached Loren. "You came?"

"Oh no," Loren said, holding up her hands as though to ward off any implication that her presence at these rituals meant something more. "I mean yes, I'm here. But I'm not . . ." She waved her hand at the initiates lining up in a procession. "I haven't made up my mind. It's a big decision, and you know I'm not good with authority. Or commitment. I can't imagine devoting my life to someone and having to do what they say for centuries. I barely managed your lessons."

If Baros was disappointed, he didn't show it. "It's not that bad. There are perks. For example, if a

Dutch woman breaks your heart, you can keep on living."

Loren smirked, but I saw her blue eyes twinkle at the Spartan's words.

As the two continued to flirt, a hush went over the room. The six gods of Olympus lined up. Actually, no. I counted five. Hera stood off to the side, her face expressionless as her brothers and sisters stood to receive the souls of the newly devoted.

In the hands of the devoted were stalks of wheat.

"You have been accepted," Demeter said, her soprano voice ringing throughout the cavern. "Today you pledge your devotion to something higher than yourself. In return, we will strengthen you on this everlasting journey. Approach and receive your blessing."

One by one, the Chosen initiates approached the gods and recited the same pledge.

"I take you to be my god, my savior. I will worship you above all others. You honor me with this special gift, and I give my soul freely for your use. Take my devotion to fuel your existence. I love what I know of you. I trust in the future that you lay at my feet. Whatsoever my life may bring to you, my soul will be at your side for all the risings and settings of the sun, for all the days of fullness and in barren times. In the foreknowledge of joy and pain, strength and weariness, I pledge myself to deepening in devotion to you, my god. My commitment is made in love, kept in faith, lived in hope, and eternally made anew."

The lights dimmed. I noted there was no electricity down here and the orbs providing luminance weren't hot. I had to assume the illumination was the work of the gods. And now that their attention was elsewhere, the glow dimmed.

The gods reached out to the humans. The humans' eyes glowed brightly until they turned white. I felt it before I saw it. The room filled with energy. It flowed freely all around, but it did not land or touch anyone.

The humans tilted their heads back and the lights went out of their eyes. The swarm of energy swelled up and into the air. Like a tidal wave, it rose. Like a tornado, it funneled down into the glowing eyes of the gods. The floor and walls hummed like an electrical overload shorting out the grid of a major city. And then, all was quiet.

It took everyone in the room a moment to catch their breaths and return to a semblance of normality.

Then Hestia came forward, as did Socrates. He was dressed in his clothes of old, his feet bare. His face looked peaceful, a small smile playing at his lips. He was flanked by two men who I knew to be Plato and Aristotle.

One by one, the gods came and shook his hand. I had to assume this was not normal because a murmur of surprise buzzed around the room at this show of gratitude from the gods. Socrates's eyes brightened while his friends' eyes dampened with tears.

Finally, the gods took their places again. Hestia hesitated, staring into her devotee's eyes. Some silent piece of communication went between goddess and Chosen. She seemed to ask him without words if he was sure. Socrates's eyelids slipped down and then rose, as though night had quickly turned to day. Looking into his empty eyes, it was clear that something new and exciting was on the horizon. He nodded to his savior.

Hestia smiled sadly. She took a deep inhale, then she nodded in acceptance. "Any final words of wisdom for us, old friend?"

"I have spent my life curved in a question mark in search of knowledge. Now I find I have come to a single point of certainty, a period in the sentence of my lifetime. To fear death, my friends, is only to think ourselves wise, without being wise; for it is to think that we know what we do not know. For anything that men can tell, death may be the greatest good that can happen to them, but they fear it as if they knew it was the greatest of evils. And what is this but that shameful ignorance of thinking that we know what we do not know?"

He'd said these words before in his past life in ancient times. They rang anew in my head. Socrates's gaze found me in the crowd, and he smiled.

"The hour of departure has arrived and, my friends, once again, we go our ways; I to die, and you to live. Which is better? Only God knows."

He embraced his ancient brothers who stood at his side. Both Aristotle and Plato's eyes glistened with unshed tears. They took hold of each of his forearms as Socrates turned back to his creator in this second life.

I thought I saw something glisten in Hestia's eyes, but she closed them before I could be sure. When she opened them again, they were glowing brightly. The energy from her went into Socrates's wide eyes. It knocked him and his companions back. Socrates's body seized. His friends caught him before he fell to the ground. When they brought him back up, he was still. His eyes were closed. A smile remained on his face.

The room was silent. The jubilation from before was dampened by the death scene before us.

Hestia stepped forward, bringing Socrates's limp body into the cradle of her slight arms.

"I'll take him, sister." Hera stepped up with her arms outstretched.

Hestia placed the deceased philosopher in her sister's arms like a sleeping baby and turned her back. This time, I was certain I saw a tear slip down the stoic goddess's cheek before she turned away.

"Let me help, my goddess," Baros offered. The ancient warrior stepped up and shouldered the weight alongside Hera.

It was unlikely that Hera needed the help, but the show of support seemed welcome. If not from her husband, who stood watching impassively, then at least from one of her husband's Chosen.

The crowd parted for Hera and Baros, allowing them a wide berth with their precious cargo. As they passed, the crowd closed. Slowly, the tension left the room and the jubilation from before crept its way back amongst the people—those long-lived and the newly reborn.

My gaze continued to stay down the hall. Baros came back within moments. But Hera was not behind him. My curiosity got the better of me, and I found myself walking down the corridor.

The passage was dark. The marble in this part of the temple was aged brown instead of pristine white. The air was damp. A fork presented itself up ahead. I wasn't sure which direction to turn. I looked behind me, preparing to give up my quest. But then I saw Hera disappearing around another corridor. My feet moved before I had a chance to think.

She was headed back in the direction of the rites, but before she got there, I watched her reach out and pull a lever. A new passageway opened. She disappeared into another doorway, and it closed behind her.

Never one to resist a hidden passageway, I stepped up to the lever and pulled. I got nothing. I patted the stone around the walls, looking to see if there was a secret handshake. Nope. I dug my nails into the crevices, but there was no give.

"Nia?"

I jerked away from the wall and turned to find Loren behind me.

"What are you doing?" she asked.

I looked back at the solid wall.

"You okay?" Loren reached out and rubbed my shoulder. "That was a bit much, watching another ancient person die."

She must've thought I was having PTSD from Vau's traumatic death. "No," I said. "I'm good. I was just checking on Hera." I looked back at the solid wall she'd disappeared behind.

"Okay, cool." Loren's voice was entirely distracted. "Listen, Lenny just invited me out for a couple of nights on his yacht. Yes, I said yacht," she squealed. "Since everything looks good here, I figured I'd go hang out for a day or two?"

"Okay," I said, still focused on Hera's disappearing act. Then I ran her words through my head again. "Wait, what happened to hoes before bros?"

"Nia, honey, I'm going to go and ride that man's boat. I suggest you do the same with a certain broody billionaire you're meeting for lunch tomorrow. Because all play and no work makes for a grumpy Nia. Girl, go get your groove back."

CHAPTER SEVENTEEN

I looked out at the Temple of Isis on the Greek island of Delos. This temple was Doric in design. The workers raised fluted columns onto rounded moldings. Under the noonday sun, sweat poured off their brown bodies. A few staggered under the weight of the stone.

I wanted to go down and lend a hand. It would take me much less effort to raise the structure with my Immortal strength. But I couldn't move. At least, I couldn't move quickly. That often happened to me when I dreamed. I was often only a viewer and not an active participant. This dream was no different.

Arms came around me. I leaned back into the cradle of his chest, in that space just below his chin and just above his heart that fit my head perfectly for centuries.

"I watched someone die last night," I said.

Zane made no sound. He only rubbed at my forearms and pressed his lips against my temple.

"He got to choose a second life, and when it ended, he got to choose when it would be over."

"Do you want that choice, *mon coeur*?"

Did I? Was I ready to die? I felt constantly weary. Had I even examined my own life? I couldn't remember over half of it. People remembered more about me than I did. Sometimes, I felt like I didn't know who I truly was.

I looked again at the temple. The workers were chiseling out the body of Isis holding the Eye of Ra. The humans were dropping to the ground as the temple structure went higher and higher into the sky.

"What's happening?" I left the cradle of Zane's protection to get a closer look.

"There is always a sacrifice to the gods," he said.

"Sacrifice?"

"The making of a deity is demanding work."

I watched the temple being built in my name rise higher, along with the body count. Leaning forward,

I saw blood pouring out of their black eyes, leaving behind a rim of red.

"I didn't ask for this," I whispered.

"They are not doing it for you, *ma petite*," he said. "They're doing it for her."

"Who?"

I turned to face Zane. He stood in profile, looking out at the horizon. I turned my head and followed the trajectory of his gaze. Floating above the temple was a woman.

"Tisa," she called. "Tisa, wake up."

She was dressed in a flowing white gown. Her wheat-colored hair rivaled the radiance of the sun. Her glowing eyes turned to me. The force of her stare knocked me back. But I didn't fall. Zane caught me.

When I could stand again, I looked out to see that we were no longer in Delos. We were standing at the foot of the Acropolis. But it wasn't the Parthenon as it stood today. This had to be one of the older versions of the building. The marble was a shiny white. There were no holes or craters. The columns stood erect and intact.

"I need you to go deeper, Tisa." The woman stood in the entryway where the statue of Athena would one day stand. "Wake up and dig deeper."

"What?" I asked. "Demeter? Is that you?"

She didn't answer. It was getting difficult to hold her gaze. Her eyes were blindingly white, like she was sucking the life out of every human whether they offered their souls freely or not.

Behind me, I felt Zane stumble. He still had a hold of me, but he let me go lest I fall to the ground with him. I turned from the floating goddess and reached out for Zane, but his fingers slipped through my grasp and he kept falling. Down into the earth he went. The ground opened and swallowed him whole.

I leaned into the crevice. But I still couldn't reach him. He seemed to fall farther and farther away from me as the ground covered him up, forming a grassy knoll over his body. I screamed his name, but no sound came from my voice.

I was wrenched awake by the sound of ringing. Sitting up in the hotel bed, I looked around wildly. The sun was shining through the window to announce a new day. The floorboards were intact with no man-swallowing hole, but I still felt unsettled.

The ringing continued until I realized it was my cell phone. I grabbed it and pulled it to my ear. "Zane?"

There was silence on the other end. "No," said the deep voice. "I'm not him."

I closed my eyes and said a silent curse. "Tres, I'm sorry. I had a nightmare—"

"No need to explain."

There was an awkward silence where I wasn't sure if it was purposeful or if the Immortal allergy was screwing with the connection. I took advantage of the hush between us to shake off the last dregs of the dream.

That was a dream, a nightmare and not reality. Zane was in Italy, likely setting up for his showing tonight. Likely not even thinking about me.

"I haven't seen or spoken to him," I said into the receiver.

"I believe you," came Tres's terse reply.

"It's just that we were together for five hundred years. It's going to take me some time to—"

"Nia."

"Yes?"

"I said, you don't have to explain."

"Okay."

I still felt like I *did* have to explain, but I'd save it for later. At the moment, I was still having trouble getting the dream out of my head.

What had the floating goddess meant as she

hovered over the Parthenon? *Dig deeper*? Had she been Demeter? She'd looked like her, but something wasn't quite right. I knew I should remember, but, as with most things in my life, I couldn't. There was just too much going on in my head.

"You didn't answer my text message," Tres said. "I'd like to see you today, if you're not out raiding tombs and saving history or whatever it is that you do."

"Despite that little knock at my profession, I'd like to see you, too." A new idea formed in my head as I spoke. But I'd need a little help putting the plan into place. Luckily, I knew just the man for the job. "Do you think we could make it a working lunch?"

Later that afternoon, Tresor Mohandis stepped out of a town car in a sleek business suit that fit his toned physique to a T. My mouth watered at the sight of him. I tugged at my lower lip as he swaggered through the tourist set. My stomach grumbled around a persistent emptiness when he came to stand before me smelling of all things edible. He carried a basket in his strong hands that smelled even better than he looked.

"When you said working lunch," he said, looking

up at the construction on the Parthenon, "did you actually mean work?"

"Only intellectually," I said.

The workers were packing up for the midday meal. I spread a picnic blanket, and Tres set down the basket of delicious scents. Then he sat, folding his long legs like a pretzel. I had to blink and then shake myself before I stretched my tongue out to get a taste of his toasty skin.

"Thanks for bringing the food," I said as I watched him unpack his bounty.

"I knew better than to rely on your cooking skills. Unless something has changed in the last millennium, I know that you're totally undomesticated."

I couldn't even take offense. He was correct. I could survive out in the wild with a dagger or even my bare hands. But put me in a kitchen and I was useless. I dug into the sandwiches he produced. The perfectly spiced bite delighted my taste buds, but the ache remained unsatisfied in my belly.

"So," Tres said, turning to me. "What are we doing here?"

I looked up at the Parthenon. "You built this temple?"

He nodded, taking a sip of bottled water.

"How many times?"

He grimaced. "Is this going to lead to another argument on sustainability, because if so—"

"No." I reached out, my fingers brushing the cotton of his cuffs. It was only a glancing touch, but I felt sparks zap across my fingertips. "No, I promise. No arguments."

Tres regarded me for a moment before answering. "Yes, I designed this building. I was in the thick of it, cutting the marble and bringing it up to the site. It took eight years to build. I consulted on the previous restoration as well. But they didn't take my advice, which only accelerated the building's demise. They've been at this particular restoration for thirty years, and they're botching it even worse."

"Why don't you offer your expertise now?"

"Not everything is meant to last, Nia. This building was modern in its time when it was built thousands of years ago. But it serves no purpose in this day except to stroke the egos of long-dead humans. If it were torn down—"

I gasped and then choked on the last bite of my sandwich.

Tres waited to be sure my airway was clear before he continued. "If it were torn down, the people alive today could use this space to improve the lives of so many in this society. The building of a new structure could support the livelihoods of hundreds."

I had nothing to say to that. The more I spoke to this man, the more his views surprised me. And worse, made sense. I'd seen him as a great destroyer, but he was a forward thinker, taking the masses into consideration.

I turned my gaze to the empty space where the statue of Athena once stood. "The gods, the Olympians, said Athena Parthenos was a mortal, one of their devotees. Did you know her?"

"I did know her." Tres chuckled, but there was no humor in his voice. "The statue that was in that building was not of Athena."

"How do you know that?"

"I know its maker. So do you."

Tres stared at me, rubbing his thumb over his lips. He didn't have to say who he meant. I knew without need of confirmation that Zane had made the statue, and that I had been his muse.

"He always seems to come between us," Tres said. "No matter what."

I'd devoured the food Tres had set before me. I'd eaten my fill, scarfing down three halves of a sandwich. And now my stomach ached for an entirely different reason.

"No, that's not true." Tres shook his head, his gaze challenging me. "He typically stays where he is. You have a habit of running back to him."

"I'm here," I insisted. "I'm not going anywhere."

Tres nodded, but it didn't look as though his movement was one of acquiescence. "You make me miss the times of the barbarians, when it was acceptable to simply tie a woman up and take her."

My breath caught. I opened my mouth to cry chauvinist, but some part of me found the thought of being at his mercy arousing. He tilted his head as though he knew it. I averted my gaze.

"Why did you bring me here, Nia? What is it you want?"

I lifted my chin. "I wanted your company."

He quirked an eyebrow.

I took a deep breath and spit it out. "And because I wanted a tour of the Parthenon—a private tour. I know there are layers. I've seen two. I'm curious if there are more."

He narrowed his gaze, and then he chuckled. "I have had women use me for my money, my contacts, but never my architectural prowess."

"Do you think you can take me down a level or two?" I asked.

"I've been trying to do that for the last millennium." He sighed, shaking his head as he gazed at me. "What have you gotten yourself into now, Dr. Rivers?"

"Nothing. Yet. Just a feeling. Do you know how to get down to the third layer?"

"Yes, I never forget a building I design. All those plans and schemes are tucked neatly in my head."

He got up and offered me his hand. I wasn't sure why I hesitated. Probably because the moment I took his palm, I felt another electric shock go through my entire body and settle deep in my core.

We stood there. Our hands were all that touched. The air was charged. Only an inch between us. He didn't lean in. Neither did I.

Tres took a step back, but as he did, he curled his fingers around mine. "Shall we?"

He didn't wait for me to answer. He gave my hand a tug. And then I was in motion.

He stayed one step ahead of me as we left the first layer of the restoration behind. He knew where the lever was to the second. Without the power of the Olympians illuminating the inner halls, we were engulfed in darkness. Immortals saw keenly in the dark, but I pulled out a flashlight from my bag as we headed down the corridor where I'd seen Hera disappear.

We came to the wall she'd disappeared behind. I pointed to the lever, but Tres was ahead of me. He reached up and pressed the space where Hera had. The passageway opened.

"Why didn't that work for me?" I asked.

"This temple once belonged to the goddess Hera. She asked me to put in a lever when the reconstruction began on the second layer."

"You knew her?"

"As much as anyone could. She was as cordial as a cactus."

He still held my hand in his as we headed down the narrow passageway. I had a mind to take it back. I didn't need his protection, but I liked the idea of being in his care. I liked the idea that he'd place me behind his strong, broad body and face any danger head-on.

"What are you hoping to find?" he asked.

"I don't know. Bodies? The Holy Grail?"

At the end of the hall was an open entryway. We entered a room. On the wall hung a large tablet. I shone my flashlight on it and gasped.

"That can't be the Holy Grail," Tres said. "Last I

heard, the Knights have it in their possession in their stronghold in Britain. And I know The Arthur would never part with it."

"It's not the Grail. It's the Ninnion Tablet."

"The what?" Tres asked.

"It was rumored to depict the rites of the Eleusinian Mysteries, but it was lost years ago."

"Are you telling me that this drawing depicts how the Olympians make demons?"

"Not demons—Chosen. The humans they take come to them freely and offer their souls. They suck the energy right out of their eyes."

"How do you know that?"

I turned to Tres. "I saw it last night."

"They invited you to see?"

I nodded. "Me and Loren."

"What?" His face contorted in horror. "Is that Van Alst woman now an immortal demon?"

"No. She declined the invitation. At least she did last night." Who knows what Baros was convincing her to do as she rode his boat.

I stared at the tablet. I had a feeling of certainty that I'd seen it before. Perhaps I'd even seen it being made?

The Ninnion Tablet was a large square plaque. Etched on it were many people, some were standing, a couple were seated. There was wheat woven throughout all the empty space in the depiction. It crowned their heads, lay at their feet, and was held in their hands like an offering.

"Huh?" I cocked my head first left and then right. My eyes darted across the picture, counting the figures once, then twice, and then, to make sure my math was right, a third time. Something didn't add up. "If this is supposed to depict the six Olympians and their rituals, why are there nine people on this plaque?"

"Are some of them humans?" Tres asked.

"I guess?" But that answer didn't feel right. Something was struggling to the forefront of my brain. There were four men and five women. But they were all wearing crowns. No human would be depicted wearing a crown.

"Is this supposed to be a depiction of the Greek gods?" Tres asked. "If so, why is the Egyptian goddess Isis depicted in here?"

"Isis?"

Tres pointed to the edge of the picture at the second seated person. Looking closely, I saw it was a woman. She sat on a throne facing two individuals, a man and a woman who were larger in stature than the others. In fact, the three of them—the large couple and the seated woman—were apart from the other six individuals, as though they were conversing in secret.

The woman in the large couple had her hand outstretched to her male partner's face, as though she was going to touch his eyes. But his body was turned away from hers. The seated woman, the one Tres pointed to as a depiction of the goddess Isis, watched the large couple before her as though in judgment. In her hands, she held a staff—the Eye of Ra.

I took a step back when I realized it was the same as the painting in my dream, the one Zane was etching. My mind went back to that dream, or perhaps it was a memory. I saw his hands working on this very piece of art. I watched his lips form an O and blow away dust as he chiseled out the staff in my hand. The same as it was in this picture. What the hell was going on?

"Do you think we can move this?" I asked Tres.

"Up three levels of narrow, crumbling temple? I'd rather not."

I took out my phone and snapped a picture. But the resulting image came out grainy. I turned on the flash and took another shot. When the light lit the room, a low moan sounded from somewhere in the corner.

Both Tres and I turned, aiming the flashlight into the corner. We were not alone. Someone cowered in the darkness.

"It's a demon," Tres said.

Tres leaped in front of me. He bent over and pulled the mass of dirty robes off the ground. Bare feet dangled. Atop the head were white wisps of hair.

"Socrates?" I asked.

But clear, pupil-less eyes full of aged wisdom and peaceful resignation didn't shine back at me. Instead, black eyes with a red rim stared. The eyes of a demon.

"But you died," I said.

"You know this thing?" Tres asked in disgust.

"Yes, that's Socrates. I watched him die last night. He'd been a devotee of the Olympians. Hestia returned his soul last night, and he died. I saw it."

"It looks like someone stole his soul back," Tres said.

I'd watched Hera take his body away. She had been stoic the whole ceremony. She had been the only god to have no new initiates.

I turned to Socrates. "Did Hera do this to you?"

Socrates opened his mouth, but he had trouble getting any words out. For a man who had spent his life debating, it broke my heart to watch him struggle with words. Finally, he was able to speak.

"Death." His hands raised to his eyes. His nails dug into his sockets. "Please."

The only way to kill a demon was through the eyes. This man had died not once, not twice, but this would be the third time. I couldn't refuse him.

"Release . . . me," Socrates begged.

"We have to set him free," I said.

"He's an empty shell. The only one who can release him is the one who stole his soul."

"There's another way." I reached to my hip and pulled loose my dagger. A strong hand came over mine. I looked up into Tres's eyes.

"I'll do it," he said.

I shook my head. "I knew him, for however briefly. I'll do it."

I cradled Socrates's head in my hands. "I'm so sorry this happened to you. I'll make her pay."

The wizened philosopher moved his lips again. It took another moment before the word would come out. "Peace," he begged.

I smiled so he'd see I had no intention of taking the high road. He opened his eyes wide to receive the relief of my dagger. I struck true twice. Instead of the celebrated sage collapsing to the ground, or trusted friend falling backward into the embrace of familiars, I caught the old man in my arms. His head rested on my chest as the life seeped out of him for the last time.

CHAPTER EIGHTEEN

Twenty minutes later, we pulled up to the hotel. We got onto the elevator and were confronted with our first problem. It required a key to get up to the penthouse and the terrace level above it where the Olympians lived.

Thank goodness I had an engineer with me. Tres opened the panel inside the elevator and did some rewiring. Within a few seconds, we were on our way up. In the confinement of the elevator, I glanced at his square jaw and curved lips, realizing how sexy math and technology were.

The door opened to the penthouse level. Three large male devotees stood on the other side of the elevator doors. They looked us up and down from their spots. With menace in their tense postures, they stepped shoulder to shoulder, blocking our path to the doors spaced out along the hall.

I took a fighting stance. There was no way I wasn't getting past them and through each one of those doors until I found Hera. She was going to pay for what she'd done to Socrates. It was three gladiator brutes against two Immortals. They didn't stand a chance. But Tres stepped in front of me.

"Trust me," Tres said. "You do not want to get on her bad side. This is between two Immortals. Let them work it out."

"What's going on out here?" Zeus emerged from behind one of the doors with a towel wrapped around his waist. His face lit up when he saw me, and the towel tented. "Nia, you're finally succumbing to my wiles."

His fiery eyes locked on Tres and his brows rose.

"And you brought a friend?" Zeus asked. "I had no idea you were so kinky."

"Where's your wife?" I growled.

Zeus grimaced. The tented towel lowered partway. "That's actually a bit kinkier than I'm comfortable with."

"I just came from the Parthenon. Socrates, the

devoted who served your family for thousands of years, was cowering in the corner as a demon."

"That's not possible." Zeus shook his head. "He was laid to rest."

"Unless someone forced him to rise, and the last person I saw with him was Hera."

"Nia?"

I turned at the sound of the lilting voice that drifted from an open door. Demeter's yellow head emerged. I rounded on her.

"Your sister made a demon out of Socrates."

Demeter's questioning smile turned upside down. "Darling, none of those words make any sense together."

"Where is she?" I stormed up to Demeter, then stepped past her. "Is she in your room?"

"No." Demeter marched backward until she blocked my path. "She is not."

"Let me see for myself."

I stepped right, but Demeter slid in front of me again. "You'll have to take my word for it, darling."

"Oh, this'll be good," Zeus said, coming closer to lean against the wall beside us, as though he wanted a front-row seat at a theatrical play.

I turned back to Demeter. She wouldn't meet my eye. "If your sister is not in there"—I pointed to the closed bedroom door—"then you'll have no problem letting me pass."

"Hera is not here. I'm in the middle of . . . private time in my room." Demeter leaned in and whispered directly in my ear, "Darling, I don't want to cause any drama in your family."

As I listened to her, I noted a tickle in my throat. Tres was behind me. Having been with him for the last few hours, my body had acclimated to his presence. It should not be having an allergic reaction so soon with just one Immortal present. Unless . . .

I turned to look behind me. Tres was grimacing, pinching the bridge of his nose as though he felt the presence of another Immortal too. I turned back to my bestie of old.

Drama in my family? Hadn't she said she preferred Zane? Did she prefer him so much she'd called him up and disappeared with him behind closed doors for some private time?

My chest burned as my heart sped up. I heard the clicking of my jaw as it clenched. My vision blurred with bright spots as I tried to bring Demeter into focus.

She was in a silk robe. The belt to the robe was haphazardly tied, revealing the top of her left thigh and the swell of her right breast. Her hair was mussed as though someone had been running their hands through it—no. *Yanking* at the loose strands. Her lips were too swollen to accomplish the grim line she was trying and failing to press them into.

"Who the hell do you have in there from my family?" I demanded.

The door creaked open. Slowly. My heartbeat slowed down until its thump reverberated in my ear. I could feel my pupils dilating as the door widened inch by inch. I looked up to see a dark head appear in the doorway.

Acid washed down my throat as a male body slid out of the opening. My gaze went fuzzy as downcast eyes appeared beneath hooded lids. He brushed his hand over his bearded chin and—

A beard? Zane couldn't abide facial hair. I slammed my eyes all the way open.

Bet. It was Bet. I took a deep breath. My heart began beating again.

Bet's shirt hung open. His pants were zipped up but unbuttoned at the top. His hair was completely disheveled. It was a bit jarring. I'd never seen him looking anything but impeccable and put together.

His gaze skated awkwardly over me and Tres, then latched onto a chuckling Zeus. He turned and glared at Demeter, accusation in his voice. "You're making demons? I should have known. Every time I let my guard down with you—"

Demeter held up a finger. "Hush, puppy."

Bet choked on the words that he had been gathering to spew forth. Like a good little pet, he heeled at her command. It was a wonder he didn't sit back on his haunches and wait for a treat. I was momentarily stunned by Demeter's power over this warlord, this conqueror of lands, this corrupter of democracy.

Demeter's attention turned to me. "Where did you see demons?"

"One demon," I said. "Socrates. He was on the third level of the Parthenon."

"Darling, Socrates was sent on to the next life. You saw it yourself." But her certainty had faltered.

I shook my head. "I saw him. His eyes were rimmed with red, and he could barely speak."

"I see." Demeter's open face slowly closed and was replaced with forced calm. "Where is he now?"

My right hand reached for my dagger. My fingertips glanced the weapon before I folded my hands in front of me. "He begged me to end his life."

Demeter reached out and took my hands in her

own. "I'm sorry you had to do that, but I thank you for taking care of the matter."

I looked into her light eyes. They were no longer bright and carefree. They had dimmed as though storm clouds had moved in.

"Well, darling." Demeter forced a smile. "I thank you for bringing this to my attention. I'll take it from here." She patted my hands and went to turn from me.

"There's more," I said. "I also saw the Ninnion Tablet down there."

"The Ninnion Tablet?" Zeus asked, coming off the wall. His handsome face had also transformed from enjoyment to concern.

"You know it?" I asked.

Neither god said anything. They remained tight-lipped and looked at each other rather than at me.

"What's the Ninnion Tablet?" Bet asked. For a man with such an impactful presence in the world, I'd forgotten he was in the room.

"The Ninnion Tablet was rumored to depict the Initiation Rites—how the Olympians granted immortality to the chosen few. But what I saw on the plaque didn't look anything like what I saw last night."

"It doesn't. It—" Zeus began, but Demeter held up her hand to stay her brother.

"There are so many depictions of us," she said, forcing a trickle of laughter that came out sounding choked. "It is but one of humanity's explanations of what they think needs to happen to become immortal."

"A human depiction?" I asked.

She swallowed, forcing her swollen lips into a thin line.

"I think I was depicted on that tablet," I said.

It was a small flicker, but I saw it pass over her features. If I hadn't already been sure, I was now that Demeter hadn't known what had happened to Socrates. But I would stake my long life on the fact that she knew something about what was going on with that tablet. Something she did not want me to know.

"Darling Tisa." Demeter took my hands in hers again. "You know we think of you as family. But you're not an actual Olympian. So it couldn't be you depicted on the plaque. Humans invented so many gods and goddesses over the years."

Her voice sounded reasonable. Like Socrates may have sounded arguing a point. But he wouldn't do that again in this life. And I knew that in another time period, I'd carried an Egyptian staff. But it had been a weapon, not a symbol of power.

"I was holding the Eye of Ra," I said.

Demeter sighed dramatically. "We've been through this. It was I who was once worshipped as the goddess Isis."

She was lying. I knew she was lying. I knew *why* she was lying. But the facts were buried beneath the layers in my mind. I saw clearly that whatever it was she was hiding, she was afraid of.

"Demeter?" I said, trying to keep my anger and frustration at bay. I didn't see a goddess before me any longer. I saw a woman who was in over her head. I just needed to know what was about to come crashing down around her. "What's going on? I keep having these dreams where you, or someone who looks like you, keeps coming to me for help."

"Dreams?" Zeus asked. "What kind of dreams?"

I opened my mouth to tell him about the dreams I'd been having where a floating woman begged me to wake up and go deeper. But Demeter let go of my hands and stepped back, blocking my view of her brother.

"This is family business, Nia. We'll find Hera and take care of her. I promise you. I'll take care of it." Her voice was choked with emotion. Her stare was full of barely contained pain. Her over-bright eyes locked on mine, pleading with me to hold my tongue about the dreams.

In the end, I gave her a slight nod of my head. But if she knew me as well as she purported to, then she'd know I had no intention of sitting on my hands and doing nothing. A flicker in her eyes told me she did indeed know this about me.

She turned back to Bet, her carefree smile back in place. "That's enough playtime today, pet. Mama has to go take care of business now. Run along with your siblings."

Bet clenched his jaw. Then he opened his mouth, but Demeter was already out the door with her own brother, disappearing into the room next door, which I had to assume belonged to another of the Olympians. Bet followed us out and into the elevator.

Once in the elevator, Bet, Tres, and I stood in a row. The elevator ride down was strained with silence. Bet took the opportunity to button up his shirt . . . and pants. Watching the kingmaker put himself back together after being dominated and discarded by the HGIC—the Head Goddess in Charge—kind of lightened the mood of death and potential destruction.

"I'm just curious," I said to Bet. "What name do you call out when you're . . . you know, in the throes of passion with our girl, Demi?"

"Good question," Tres said. He tapped his bottom lip in serious thought. "Because he couldn't call out *Demeter*."

"No." I shook my head. "Because that would give her more power, as he said."

"Do you suppose he calls out *god*?"

"Enough," Bet bellowed.

Instead of being cowed, Tres and I snickered. Who could blame us? This man who'd leveled barbarians, generals, and politicians alike was trying to cover bite marks on his neck by turning up his rumpled shirt collar. He could not be taken seriously at the moment.

"I was here working out a way for this infernal country to get out of debt," he said.

"Infernal?" I said. "Is that what the kids are calling it these days?"

Tres snorted. Bet cut me with his eyes.

I decided to give it a rest. Bet might have a few of the answers that Demeter wasn't willing to give up.

"You said they'd made demons before?" I asked Bet.

"It was long ago, back in Egypt. During the time

when their parents were still alive. I remember whole tribes and cities falling prey to their idea of *worship*." Bet sneered.

Whole cities?

"But it stopped once they came to Greece and their parents were laid to rest," Bet continued.

"Their parents died here?"

Bet shrugged. "I don't think they ever actually died. They just disappeared one day and were never seen again. It was her father, Cronus, that I'd mainly had the problem with. I tried to make peace with him a few hundred years before the Battle of Thermopylae. But he refused. All of this could've been avoided if he'd simply accepted the treaty."

"Oh, I see," Tres said. "That's what you were doing just now in her bedroom with your clothes off —making a treaty."

Bet turned to glare at Tres. Tres looked over at Bet with faux innocence. The elevator dinged and the doors opened. Bet stormed out. Tres laughed behind him. Though I saw the humor, I couldn't bring myself to laugh. Something was going on in that family.

"Just goes to show you," Tres said.

"Show what?"

"That if you have that much venom for someone, there's usually something deeper there."

"You think that's love between Bet and Demeter?"

"Whatever it is between them, it's a damn thin line."

He looked at me pointedly. There had been the same level of venom between us over the years. But we hadn't started wars to antagonize each other. Maybe a few international incidents, but no one had died.

"You're not going to let this go, are you?" Tres asked as we stepped into the hotel lobby.

I shook my head. Then I crossed my arms over my chest and prepared for an argument.

"Fine." He sighed, reaching out a hand and tracing the fine hairs between my temple and my ears. "I have business to attend to in Crete. I'll be back in two nights."

He leaned down and touched my lips with his. It was a brief contact. But the impact made me lose my balance. I fell into his chest. Instead of pulling me closer, he held me up by the elbows until I regained my balance.

"Don't do anything stupid," he said once I was steady and standing on my own.

"I make no promises."

I watched him walk out the door of the hotel. When he was out of sight, I went back inside the elevator and pressed the button to my floor. Once in my room, I grabbed the dress Demeter had gifted to me, along with my travel bag. Then I headed to the airport to do something stupid.

CHAPTER NINETEEN

I stepped out of the cab onto the narrow street. The streets of Rome were packed this evening with tourists and young partygoers. I headed in the opposite direction from the restaurants and nightclubs. After opening the doors of the art museum, I walked into a room filled with the upper crust of art snobbery.

"Look at his use of Conté," said one woman with feathers in her hair. She puffed up her chest as she used the artsy-fartsy term for what amounted to a crayon. "It's so playful and whimsical."

"It's as though he's deconstructing what it means to be a child but through the eyes of a man," said a rotund man. His chubby fingers hovered over the lines of the art piece.

They were both wrong. Zane's work was always straightforward. He didn't believe in the metaphysical. He didn't often wax philosophical. He simply saw something he thought was beautiful and captured that moment in time to make it a permanent fixture for generation after generation to see.

This was the showing he'd missed two months ago when he came to be with me in Beijing and then to the Gongyi to save me from a horde of assassins known as the Lin Kuie, or forest ghosts.

On the walls, I recognized parts of my body in the landscapes, textures, and colors. In the sculptures, I saw the same. Given that I was his favorite subject to draw, paint, and mold, I didn't have to look too hard to find my likeness.

Neither did I have to look hard to find him.

In the center of the room was a makeshift dance floor. A few couples swayed to the band. Zane held a woman in his arms. She tilted her head back in laughter, exposing her long neck to him.

Her breasts pushed up, but Zane's gaze remained hooded, which wasn't hard. His lashes were so long and thick it was often hard for others to tell if they had his full attention or not.

I'd never had to question if I had his attention.

Whenever I came into the room, his gaze would always find me. Right now, his eyes stayed locked on the woman in his arms.

But I knew he knew I was there. Not just because of the Immortal allergy. Even when we'd spent days, weeks together, to the point we were both sniffling and growing weak, he always looked up and caught sight of me the moment before I stepped into his view. I could never surprise him. He knew my moves before I made them.

On the dance floor, Zane pressed his partner into his torso. With the practiced grace of someone who had danced at balls for centuries, he spun the woman around so his back was to me. The woman's hand traced down to his tight ass. My vision went red.

I marched through the dancers on the floor. A few couples stumbled as they moved to get out of my way. I didn't stop my advance until I was standing shoulder to shoulder with the woman in Zane's arms. I glared daggers at her. She was lucky I didn't put one through her wayward hand.

The woman blinked her muddy-brown eyes at me. "Is there a problem?"

"You're in my spot," I hissed.

She laughed and looked to Zane. When he said

nothing, she turned back to me, but spoke to him. "What is she? A crazed fan of yours?"

"It would appear so, yes?" He chuckled. "I can feel her nostrils flaring behind my back. I'm sure her eyes are glaring daggers at you. Careful, she likely has one or two strapped to her thigh."

His voice was a purr, as though he liked the thought of the jade blade that was indeed strapped to my right thigh. The metamorphic rock wasn't something TSA looked for in their security checks, allowing me to carry it around the world with ease. I didn't think I was in any danger here in Rome. It was just a habit that I went everywhere with a weapon strapped to my body.

Realizing she might be in danger, the woman in Zane's arms stilled. "What the hell? Is this your wife or something?"

"No," Zane said. Though I couldn't see his face, I heard the smile in his voice. "She is my muse, my goddess, my soul mate. She is the reason I wake up each morning and can see the beauty in the world. I capture it not for the eyes of you or any other patrons. I capture it so she can see how beautiful the world is with her in it."

The woman gaped at Zane's face as he continued to hold her in his embrace. I gaped at his back as he delivered the poetic lines like a romantic calling up to my balcony. So maybe he did wax a little philosophical from time to time.

I didn't soften at his words. I remained tense. He still held the woman in his arms, swaying slightly. It was seriously pissing me off.

"But," Zane continued, "she is cross with me for keeping secrets. Perhaps enough time has passed that she is ready to forgive?"

He turned his head, but not enough for his dark gaze to connect with mine. In his peripheral vision, he must've found his answer. He sighed, his shoulders slumping forward. "That feels like a no."

He looked down at the woman he still held in his arms. He continued to sway, but she was now as still as one of his statues. "You should probably go," he said to her. "This is likely to get ugly."

The woman ducked out of his embrace and skittered away without looking back. I watched her go, still seething with jealousy, which was insane. I'd never once felt jealous when it came to Zane. I'd never once doubted his fidelity and devotion to me.

But that was in the past. We weren't together anymore. He could do whatever he wanted with whomever he wanted.

This trip had been a mistake. A big, stupid

mistake. I prepared to head for the exit to the museum. But that was when he turned.

His gaze dipped to the floor, beginning with my shoes. Those soulful eyes traveled up my legs, prominently displayed in the short cocktail dress. It was a slow perusal. I held still. I always held still for him. Time ceased to move. The world stopped spinning. Nothing mattered when I was with Zane except the moment we were in.

Finally, he reached my face. His dark eyes caressed every inch of my skin, looking for a new angle, searching out a new shade.

"*Bonsoir, ma petite nova.*"

His voice was a caress. It reached out and wrapped itself around me. I felt it pulling me to him. In that moment, I couldn't remember why I was resisting this familiar place where I loved to be. I reached into my shoulder bag and felt for my cell phone. The feel of the device cradled in my hand reminded me of my purpose here.

"I'm not here for a social visit," I said.

"Business then?" He grinned. "Have you come to patronize my work?"

"Yes, actually. That's exactly why I'm here."

"Take whatever you want." Zane waved his hand around the room filled with high-priced art. "Or, better yet, let me make you something new."

I was immobile in the middle of the dance floor as his words tried to sway me. But I could not be moved. I had a purpose here. I shook my head to bring my mission back into focus. I looked down so his lazy grin would stop clouding my concentration.

I pulled out my phone. After tapping a few keys, I held it up in front of him. "Is this your work?"

Quick as a snake, Zane reached for my wrist. The moment his fingers touched my skin, I shuddered. I dropped my phone into his hand and yanked away from his grasp. His gaze locked on me and lit with amusement before it went to the phone's screen.

Zane frowned. "I cannot see anything. It's all dark. You know I'm not one for the abstract, Nova."

I took the phone back from him and peered at the device's face. On the screen was the picture I'd snapped of the Ninnion Tablet. But it was the first snapshot, the one in the dark. I swiped to the second image I'd taken. The one where I'd used the flash that had startled Socrates. The thought of Socrates and his red-rimmed gaze steeled my resolve. I handed the phone back to Zane.

"It's the Ninnion Tablet," I said. "It depicts the Eleusinian Mysteries."

"Yes, I know," Zane said. "I carved it for you."

"For me?"

He nodded. "You asked me to make this scene for you. You gave me all the details—the Olympians and their parents."

So the other two people in the tablet aside from me were Cronus and Rhea, their not-quite-dead parents.

"You asked me to add the wheat," Zane continued. "And you asked me to add your likeness as well." He pointed to the corner of the picture where the woman sat with the Eye of Ra.

Part of me wanted to call up Demeter and tell her *I told you so*. I was the goddess Isis, not her. But now wasn't the time.

"I asked you for this?"

Zane nodded, handing the phone back to me. "I made it for you, maybe fifteen hundred years ago."

"Did I say why I wanted it made? What it meant? Why I asked you to depict me in a piece with Greek gods?"

"No, but I suppose it had something to do with your argument with Demeter. And before you ask, no, you didn't tell me what the argument was about."

"I just asked you to create a cryptic piece of artwork and gave you no clue as to why?"

Zane shrugged. "It wasn't the first time."

"And you did it without asking?"

"Of course," he said. "Why wouldn't I?"

"It clearly means something. Weren't you curious what I was hiding?"

"You keep a lot of secrets, *mon coeur*. You keep them *for* others and you keep them *from* others. I trust that if you need me to know something, you'll tell me. I won't interfere unless I feel you might be in danger."

There was a pregnant pause as we both thought about the Lin Kuie and the danger that had come after the secrets we'd both kept in that instance.

"And," Zane continued, "if you needed me to help you hide something, even if it was from yourself, then I'd have done so."

I stared at this man. He watched me patiently. There was an inch of air between us, but he took no steps to close the distance. Zane never made advances. He always waited for me to make a move. He stood still now, eyes drinking me in, nostrils flaring, lips parted—waiting.

"Will you dance with me, Nova?"

"No," I said. My palms went sweaty, and I had to put my phone into my shoulder bag lest it fall to the floor. "I'm working. I have to get back to Greece."

He nodded. He was close enough for me to smell the wine on his breath. When he exhaled again, the alcohol sailed through my nostrils, leaving me feeling lightheaded. My lips parted, waiting for another hit.

"Are you trying to recover the tablet?" he asked.

"Hmm?" I tilted my head up and nearly bumped his chin. "No, I know where it is. I just don't know what it means."

Though with the pieces of the puzzle falling together, I could see I knew not only the Olympians, but also their Titan parents. And with the parents standing so close to me on the tablet, I had to assume I knew something more than the offspring.

But my brain was having trouble focusing on ancient gods at the moment. Zane was so close I could hear his heart beating in his chest. I felt my body swaying to the beat of the music, or was it the beat of his heart?

"I'm sorry I cannot help you with your mystery," he said into my ear. "Perhaps if you made up with Demeter, she might tell you?"

I placed my hand on his chest to push him away. But I'd forgotten how soft that space between his pecs was, how perfectly my head fit there. "Demi and I are good."

"That's good." His voice sounded above me. His chin rested on the top of my head. "It's good to forgive friends."

My thighs brushed against his. My other hand came to rest on his hip. His hand mirrored mine and rested on my hip. His fingers spanned my lower back as we swayed to the beat.

I'd said I wouldn't dance with him. I wasn't really sure how I ended up in his arms. All the weariness I'd felt for the last two months vanished as I rested my head against his chest. I'd just stay here for a few minutes more, just to rest. And then I'd be off to do what I was supposed to do.

Just a few minutes more...

CHAPTER TWENTY

One moment resting on Zane's chest turned into one dance. One dance turned into two. When the music stopped hours later, we were still in motion, but now we were moving onto the street. And then up an elevator. Down a hall. And through a door.

I was just going to go in and talk to him. To give him a piece of my mind about his silence for the last two months. But when I closed the door behind us and opened my mouth to confront him, somehow my tongue got tied up. In his mouth.

I meant to pull away. To start again, correctly this time. By using my words. But my stomach grumbled, and I remembered how hungry I was. How hungry I'd been for weeks.

As I pulled his lower lip into my mouth, I began feeling a sense of fullness. The thirst that had parched my throat was quenched. The craving for something savory was satisfied as he licked into my mouth.

I was going to let him go. I was going to stop this madness. As soon as I was full.

In the meantime, I took my fill. I attacked his lips. There were no dainty sips on my part. I sealed my lips with his and plundered, gulping him down.

He allowed it. He opened himself up to me fully as I drank him in. It felt as though I was pulling from him. He felt boundless, bottomless, as he let me take in his essence, drawing his life force from him. But it wasn't enough. Just as soon as I became sated, I wanted more.

Zane pulled away from me. I dug my nails into his back, not willing to let him go. It didn't appear he had any intentions of going far. He sank to his knees, my dress coming with him.

I retracted my claws from his skin to allow the garment to fall to the floor. He reached for the dagger strapped at my hip. Looking up at me before he touched the blade, he quirked an eyebrow for permission.

Here was my chance. My chance to say no. This had already gone further than I had planned.

Zane stood and backed from me, leaving the dagger in place. He rubbed his thumb at his lower lip, his hooded gaze soaking me up. "*Mon dieu.* You against the skyline of Rome . . . it's breathtaking. Just let me sketch it."

The lights were out in his room. The only illumination came from the picture window at my back. I could imagine what I looked like standing in heels, a thong, and a blade strapped to my thigh.

Demeter had been right about this dress and my breasts. A bra had been unnecessary. My nipples were aching with the need to be held, kissed, tasted.

But instead of coming closer to do any of those things, Zane took another step back. And then another. From my place against the skyline of an ancient city, I knew where Zane's body was headed.

Before he could reach for his pencil and pad, I was on him. His body was turned from me. I took hold of the back of his shoulders. Gripping him, I tossed his body back. He went airborne and landed on the large bed at the center of the room.

He landed with an *oomph.* He tried to rise, but I climbed over him and shoved him back down onto the mattress. He threw his head back and let out a deep- bellied laugh as I pinned his forearms down with my knees.

"*D'accord, ma petite*," he chuckled. "The art can wait."

Damn straight the art would wait. But I couldn't. I needed to possess this man. I ripped at his shirt until I felt his flesh beneath my nails. He groaned against my mouth as our teeth mashed together. I watched him wince in pain, but he didn't stop me.

"Whatever you need, *mon coeur*. Take from me."

I had to stop his lips from moving. I needed them on me, against me. Open for me to drink, to taste, to take.

My hands went to his pants. I fumbled with his buckle. Frustrated, I released the dagger from its holster. His eyes widened and his grin kicked up. I sliced through the leather with a flick of the blade, then tossed the leather strap and the jade blade to the ground. I slid the slacks down his strong thighs while I attacked his mouth once more. When my hands couldn't go further, I used my bare feet to free his shins and his feet until he was bare for me, an offering.

My hands tracked up his thighs and met warm, throbbing flesh. My mouth watered, my gut tightened around emptiness, as though I hadn't been taking everything this man had given me. I reared back from him, breathing in shallow pants.

What was I doing? This had gone further than I had intended. I'd just meant to ask him a few questions. How had he ended up beneath me? How had I ended up on top of him, naked?

Zane lay beneath me, still and patient even as his erection throbbed between us. His arms were stretched over his head, gripping the headboard of the hotel bed, as though he knew if he let go, he would take me.

Why didn't he just take me? He could have his way with me if he chose. I could see through the haze of desire in his eyes; he needed me to choose him. He needed me to take this step toward him.

I didn't want a choice right now. My mind was all wrong. I didn't want to do the right thing, which I knew was to get out of this bed and stop screwing around with my ex.

The problem was that, for me, it would just be a step. For him, it would be as though I leaped back into his arms, and I wasn't sure I wanted to do that. I just needed this moment. I'd felt so lost for the last few weeks. I'd had people telling me about a me that I couldn't remember, a me I was no longer in touch with. I just needed to cling to the familiar, to what I knew.

I was starving, parched, so in need of what he could give me. I knew that things weren't repaired between us. An eternity that I couldn't remember, past lives and deeds that he'd kept from me, still raged between us. But not in this moment. It was just me and him. Nia and Zane. It made sense, and I needed it right now.

It was selfish, childish, and immature. But I didn't care. I aimed his cock for my entrance and sank down onto him.

Zane's eyes closed in a silent prayer of gratitude. With my decision made, he let go of the headboard and latched onto me. He grabbed my ass and rocked into me. Slowly at first. But that only lasted a few strokes, and then he lost his control.

I wrapped my arms around his shoulders and attacked his mouth. We clung to each other, exploring the spots the other liked. Sucking at the places we knew were sensitive. Angling our thrusts in the ways we would drive each other wild.

All the while, Zane whispered prayers both new and familiar in my ear. I felt refueled by his worship. I was rejuvenated by his devotion. And when I reached my climax, I felt sated by his offering.

CHAPTER TWENTY-ONE

I heard the *scritch-scritch* against parchment at my back. The sound of Zane drawing was a constant in my sleeping and waking hours. I didn't want to open my eyes from this dream and confront the day. But the voice found me anyway.

"Tisa, I cannot wait much longer. I need you to wake up."

From the darkness of my dreams, the floating woman stepped in front of me. "Demeter?"

I peered at the woman. She did favor Demeter with the wheat-colored hair and sparkling eyes. But there was something . . . different about her. I couldn't put my finger on it.

"I need you to remember my birth," she said. "Remember before it's too late."

"Your birth?"

"You don't have much time. They are gathering. You need to wake up."

But I didn't want to wake up. I didn't want her in my dreams anymore, disturbing my peace. The moment I thought it, she was gone.

Had I known it was that easy to get rid of a floating Greek goddess, I would've done it a week ago. I sighed and snuggled deeper into the pillows as the scene changed before my eyes.

Sun kissed my eyelids and brought to mind the sight of an ancient city. I saw domed steeples reaching into the morning sky and the Flavian Amphitheater of Rome stretching up. But there was a portion of the circular Colosseum that was damaged.

Behind me, I again heard the markings of long lines and circles as Zane continued his artwork. I didn't want to turn around. I always woke from the dream when I moved.

As I lay still, I realized I missed having his heat at my back. I missed the sounds his pencils and brushes made against parchment. I held still in the dream and let the familiar sounds lull me deeper into relaxation. Looking out at the Colosseum, I remembered a time long ago.

"You took me on a date there," I said.

"*Oui, mon coeur*. We saw the gladiators."

I remembered. We'd sat upon cushioned curules —folding chairs—in a section for the elites. I remembered the gladiators. Their glistening, muscled skin. The clangs of their swords and armor. I remembered the sweat pouring off their bodies, the blood spraying from their wounds. As someone used to death, the violent display hadn't unnerved me. What had turned my stomach was the reaction of the crowd.

The hunger and glee of those gathered to watch the display, their insatiable appetite for more carnage, had made me turn away. I had shut my eyes and placed my hands over my ears to tune them out.

Closing my eyes to the building that was out the window, I concentrated instead on the scratch of pencil against paper.

"I feel I'm constantly watching things, people, places, get destroyed," I said. After a moment, I opened my eyes again to view the ruined structure. I felt like I was looking through a window of time, seeing the building in its prime and after its destruction. "Tres says he rebuilds to keep things moving, but I don't believe him. I think he does it to cover up the past."

"Tres?"

"Did you know he built on top of the Parthenon? And the city of Troy. I wonder if he built the Colosseum, too?"

Zane's pencils went silent behind me. My past with Tres was a bone of contention between us. But it was my dream. I could say whatever I wanted.

"I think you two would get along if you tried," I said.

"We used to get along very well."

"What happened?" I knew the answer before he said it.

"He desires to possess the very thing that makes my heart beat. So we no longer see eye to eye."

I looked again at the damaged roof of the once-great building. A plane flew overhead. The sounds of car horns honking in the distance sounded loud in my head. What a vivid dream this was.

Somewhere nearby, a cell phone rang. That was odd for a dream. Out of the corner of my eye, I spied a rectangular device vibrating on the bedside table. I raised my head from the pillow in my dream to see Tres's name on the screen.

I sat up.

I turned to look behind me.

Zane lounged like a large cat with his back against the headboard. His gaze soaked me up as his pencils worked on parchment.

"Oh no," I groaned.

This wasn't a dream. I was in Rome, in bed, with my ex.

"*Bonjour*," he said.

Looking down, I saw that only the sketchpad covered Zane's manhood.

"Oh no," I wailed.

How had this happened? I had only come to ask him a question, which, yes, I could have asked on the phone. But technology was always weird between Immortals. Even so, I still could've come to the exhibit, gotten my answer, and left. That had been the plan. I didn't have to dance with him. Or kiss him. Or sleep with him. Granted, I didn't remember much sleeping happening.

I groaned again. "This wasn't supposed to happen. I tipped you over."

"Yes, you did." Zane grinned.

"No, I mean you as the refrigerator."

"Pardon?"

"Our relationship. You're my refrigerator. I tipped

you over already. You're on the ground, and I'm standing over you."

"I don't understand."

"I didn't mean to sleep with you."

He nodded with fake apology. "Well, you could've stopped the second time. Or, perhaps, the third go-around."

"Zane!" I pulled the pillow over my head as though no one could see me. Then I realized that no one could. No one needed to know this had happened.

The moment the thought came it eased my mind. His phone rang. I pulled the pillow from my head to see him lean over and look at the caller ID. Then he picked it up.

I stared at him in a bit of shock. He never took calls when we were together. Who the hell was on the other end of the line who was so important?

"*Allo.*" He smiled into the phone.

I couldn't hear what the other person said, but I knew it was a woman. Femininity wafted out of the receiver like a cheap perfume.

Zane chuckled, his face pressed against the handheld device. I was seething by the time he turned to me. I'd completely forgotten my ire about last night now that his attentions were elsewhere this morning.

"It's for you." He handed me his phone.

I took it and placed it to my ear. "Hello?"

"You slut."

I shut my eyes and let my head sink into my free hand. "How'd you know I was here?"

"I looked in the closet of your hotel room," Loren said. "One: only the sexy dress was gone. Two: Tres left a message at the front desk asking to see you tomorrow night, so I assumed you weren't with him. And three: I also noted that your passport was gone."

"I thought you were with Baros for another night."

"He got called in by his keeper." She huffed. "Apparently, they've found Hera. Thought you might like in on that action. I heard what she did to Socrates. I'm sorry."

"I'll be back in a couple of hours."

"Hmm? Gonna fit in one more quickie before your flight?"

"Shut up." I jabbed my thumb into END and tossed Zane's phone on top of the comforter.

I turned and faced him. Then I pulled the covers around my chest so he'd focus on me and not my breasts.

"Zane, this was . . ." What? A mistake? Me using him to feel better about myself? Just a one-night stand with the person I'd loved for longer than I could remember?

"Let me guess," he said. "You're not ready to be back in a relationship."

I shook my head.

"You got caught up in the moment. Things were familiar and comfortable. And you let things happen that you now regret."

"I don't regret it."

And I didn't. I also didn't appreciate him telling me about myself, like I didn't know who I was. Just like everyone around me had been doing this past week. Especially when he was the one who knew me best because he had been there for me for the last five hundred years, but not in the last five weeks.

"Why haven't you called me?" I demanded.

"Because you prefer to have space when we break up."

I had to unclench my teeth before I could speak. "*When we break up*? You say that like it's a thing that we do on a regular basis. Like, *Hey Nia, do you want to go to the movies this weekend? And then afterward, maybe we can break up for a century or so.*"

Zane's gaze narrowed on me, which was hard to

do with his thick lashes and squinty eyes. "Yeah, that sounds about right."

I stared at him, incredulous. "And then you just leave me alone until I forget again?"

"No. I am never far from you. I always come when you need me."

"Like a stalker."

He took a deep breath and pinched the bridge of his nose. As I'd mentioned, Zane and I had been together for a long time. We'd had more than our fair share of arguments. He'd typically close his eyes when I was on his nerves. He'd pinch the bridge of his nose when he was at the end of his rope. I was two for two today.

"When I chase you," he said, "you run. When I give you space, you hunt me down. Why don't you just tell me what you want me to do this time?"

"I don't know what I want you to do." I stood and stomped my foot. Then I wrapped my arms around my naked torso. "I don't know what I want. I'm obviously confused. The only thing I know for sure is that I don't want to hurt you."

Zane took a deep breath. He stood, too. We both stood there, naked from our lovemaking the night before. Irritated under the hazy cloud of the morning after.

Zane rocked back on his heels. My breath caught at the thought of him actually tipping over, like a refrigerator I had no more use for. I reached my hand out as though to catch him. His fingers snaked out and grabbed my wrist. He pressed his chest into my palm. I felt his heartbeat against my fingertips.

"It only hurts when you forget me," he said.

"I won't ever do that again, I swear." I took a step into him. "I think you're my best friend in the entire world."

"I am. Through the universe and all of time."

I sighed and rested my head on the space that was uniquely mine, that space between his pecs. "Don't tell Loren I said that. She might claw your eyes out if she thinks you're blowing up her spot."

Zane chuckled. The puffs of air felt good on my face.

"No matter what happens between us," I said, "that's never going to change. We'll always be friends."

"Yes," he said. "I suppose that will never change. Unless, of course, I commit another mass genocide in your name."

"Yeah, so let's not do that."

I felt his cheeks spread in a grin against my temple.

"I really do have to go," I said.

"Right." Zane released me. "An archaeologist's work is never done."

"Not until the end of time."

I looked up at him. He peered down at me. We stood before each other, baring more than our souls. There was still an ocean between us, but at least he was close enough for me to see, to touch, to talk to.

"So we're good?" I asked.

"You mean with this undefined non-relationship where we may or may not see each other, but will remain secret besties through all time? Yeah, sure, we're good."

"Good."

CHAPTER TWENTY-TWO

The moment the seat belt light went off in the commercial aircraft, I got up. I moved easily through the crowded plane as I had no luggage to carry off. All my gear was slung over my shoulder in an overnight bag. It was the baggage I carried on the inside that bothered me. It wasn't a light load.

Aside from a general achiness from being exposed to three Immortals in one day, my lips still stung from the lingering kiss Zane had given me as I stood on the other side of the threshold of his hotel room. My body ached with the memories of his attention from the previous night. My palm itched over the unanswered text messages from Tres. My head hurt as I tried to figure out what to say when I saw him next. At customs, I had nothing to declare so they let me pass.

Up ahead in the arrivals, I heard a commotion. A group of young coeds were whooping and high fiving at the end of the long hallway. When I got closer, I saw the reason and nearly turned away to board another flight.

Loren stood with a sign that read *High fives if you got some last night.*

An old woman with silver-white hair made her way over and gave Loren a high five. The cougar was accompanied by a much younger man. The crowd went wild.

And then Loren spotted me.

"Rome to Athens?" she said, holding up her hand for a slap. "I think that must be one of the longest morning-after walks of shame I've ever witnessed."

"Shut up," I growled, ignoring her outstretched hand.

Instead, I reached into my pocket to retrieve my vibrating phone. I took one look at it before shutting it down and shoving it back in my pocket. This time in my back pocket instead of the front.

"Is that the Broody Billionaire? Did you tell him

you and Frenchie were rocking the refrigerator last night?"

"Loren..." I sighed, pinching the bridge of my nose.

"Hey," called one of the noisy coeds. He broke away from the whooping and hollering and came to stand before Loren. "Come hang out with us tonight. We're headed to this wild party. Free booze, a little recreational medicine ..."

He held up a printed sheet of paper. It had the same wheat wreath image that our invitations had, the ones to the Mysteries that Baros had given us in Budapest. But unlike ours, this invite was in black and white, not gold-embossed lettering or expensive paper stock. It also had the addition of a peacock plume in the middle of the wreath, like the one that had been discarded by the dejected partygoer who hadn't been able to gain access to Zeus's orgy.

"Wild party, huh?" Loren took the invitation out of his hands and held it up for further inspection.

"Yeah," the guy said. "It's gonna be down in Eleusis. I'd never heard of the place, but it's not that far from Athens."

"Where'd you get this invitation?" I asked.

"It's all over social media," he answered. His eyes were on Loren, not me. "So, you'll show?"

"Maybe." She tossed the comment, and her sign, over her shoulder as we set into motion toward the exit. Once there was distance between us, she said, "Do you think it's still our friendly neighborhood scammer who's doing those invitations?"

"I don't know. He didn't look like he had a big operation. Those kids are international."

"You do know that the internet is worldwide?" she said. "Baros and I were headed toward Eleusis when we got the call that they'd found Hera."

"What were you planning to do in Eleusis?"

"Besides him?" Loren crossed her arms over her chest, fingers clenched in a fist.

"I take it your little getaway didn't go as planned?"

Her face screwed in frustration. I heard the tendons in her neck as she rolled her head around. "He took me on a tour of the great battles of the Spartans. We started in Thermopylae. Where he died. How sexy is that?"

It didn't sound to me like the question needed a response, so I kept my mouth shut.

"There I was, in a barely-there bikini, and he's going on about battles he'd fought thousands of years ago, like we were watching a highlights reel of the last fifty years of the World Cup."

"I guess once a military and political mastermind, always a military and political mastermind."

Loren cut me with her eyes. "Not when you have a naked and willing woman spread out in front of you."

We stepped out of the sliding glass doors and into the cool Athens air. The sun was moving lower toward the horizon. Tourists were pouring into the city, looking for excitement and adventure, as the residents were getting off work and preparing for relaxation and family time.

It should have been a typical weekday evening in the city. But I felt something in the air. It felt like the ground was humming with energy. There was a buzzing, much like what I'd experienced at the Chosens' rites a couple of nights ago. But the Olympians weren't doing another rite tonight. They were interrogating their wayward sister.

"I don't know what's going on," I said. "But something doesn't feel right."

"Let's get to the hotel," Loren said. "Maybe the answers are there."

We hailed a taxi at the curb and hopped in.

"What else did you find out?" I asked. "Did Baros

say whether Hera put up a fight when they found her?"

Loren shook her head. "When I spoke to him, he said she walked in the door and sat down to breakfast with her siblings. He said they were talking like civilized people. That's when I knew he was lying. What family is civilized at the dinner table?"

We arrived at the hotel. With my memory of Tres's wiring trick, the elevator took us up to the penthouse. The door to the Olympians' stronghold was unguarded, but I felt a tickle at my throat.

I steeled myself to face Tres, but standing in the corner was Bet. At the opposite end of the wall was Baros. The large warrior's black gaze was trained on Bet. I could hear his molars grinding from where I stood. He cracked his knuckles one by one, pressing against the digits. The crunching sound filled the silent hall.

For his part, Bet leaned casually against the wall. He either didn't notice Baros throwing optical daggers at him or he did and put on airs to get a rise out of the Spartan warrior.

It was possible Bet had forgotten about his hand in the demise of Leonidas and the Spartans. Or, more likely, he was relishing rubbing the man's ancient defeat in his face. In hand-to-hand combat, I'd put my money on Bet. In a battle of wills, he'd be my pick for odds as well. Bet's age, experience, and strength were no match for a warrior even as great as King Leonidas.

"What are you doing here?" I asked Bet. "And why are you hanging around outside the door?"

His smirk turned downward at the question. "Demeter kicked me out. Family business, she said."

I stared. Was that a pout on the second oldest Immortal's face? Was he spinning his wheels over the rejection of a woman? This day just kept getting weirder and weirder.

Bet turned to Loren. "Aw, you went and got yourself another pet, Tisa?"

Loren bristled. Baros used that as an excuse to step away from his corner. I went to step between all three of them, not sure whom I would be guarding from whom, when shouting rose from behind the closed door of Demeter's apartment.

"How could you do that, Hera?"

Four heads turned to the door. I tried it and found it unlocked. After I turned the knob and opened it, we all filed in. Hestia was speaking as we entered. It was the most animated I'd seen the serious woman this week.

"Socrates never did anything to you," Hestia said. "Or is this about me? Are you still mad about Hippocrates?"

Hera sat in the center of a sofa. Demeter faced her in a high-backed chair. Hestia stood on one side of Demeter, Hades stood on the other. Poseidon hung back, looking out a window. Zeus leaned against the wall behind Hera.

In answer to Hestia's question, Hera rolled her head around her neck and looked up from her solitary seat. She glared her golden eyes at her sister.

"He only gave me his soul," Hestia said, placing her hands on her hips in a defensive move. "But you clearly had his heart. Give me the word and I'll call him back from the World Health Organization."

"It's not about you, Hippocrates, or Socrates." Hera's voice was dispassionate as she gazed out the window at the setting sun on the Acropolis.

"Oh, Hera." Demeter rose from her throned chair and came to sit down next to her sister.

Once seated, Demeter reached out her hands to Hera's. Hera looked over at her sister in surprise. Slowly, her fingers stretched to life and began to curl around Demeter's. But before Hera's fingers finished the embrace, Demeter pulled away.

"It's about me, isn't it?" Demeter asked.

Hera's face shuttered like blinders in a sudden storm. She shrugged her sister's hands off her person and went to the window.

"Of course it's not about either of you," Zeus heckled from his spot against the wall. "She's obviously doing it to get my attention. Although why I would care what she does with a seventy-year-old, I have no idea."

"Oh, shut up, you ass." Hera's cool countenance broke and she whirled on Zeus, eyes crackling.

Zeus met her thunderous gaze with one of his own. The very humidity in the room changed as the two faced off from opposing ends of the room. It felt cold, warm, and damp all at the same time.

Hera broke the stare off first. Her beautiful face contorted into something ugly as she turned her glare on the rest of her siblings. "You all expect me to be content with my lot in life. Just to pick up your scraps."

"What scraps?" Demeter asked, rising from the couch. "Hera, you're worshipped by millions."

"No one chooses me. Not humans, not any of you. You all take from me, but no one stays."

She turned her glare back on Zeus. "For hundreds of years, I've felt like I've been walking around on fumes. I just want something of my own. Do you have any idea how hungry I am?"

They stared at her in confusion. I felt sorry for her. She had a close-knit family to lean on, but she felt like an outcast in the crowd.

"You're being dramatic as always," Zeus said. "You should've been the patron saint of the theater instead of mothers. You're exactly like the symbol the humans gave you—a peacock who shakes its big bright tail feathers to get attention."

My ears perked up at the mention of the peacock. Then it hit me. Each of the Greek gods had symbols to identify them. Zeus had his thunderbolt. Poseidon his trident. Hades his scepter. Hestia's was the hearth. Demeter's was wheat. And Hera's . . . was the peacock.

"Or better yet," Zeus was saying, or rather, shouting, "I should've left you in our father's belly after he swallowed your essence."

His siblings' heads all snapped to him at the mention of their parents.

"I wish you had," Hera said. "At least *he* wanted my love."

Like in a tennis match, everyone's heads snapped back across the room to her.

"Darling, no." Demeter insinuated herself

between the two raging gods. "He didn't want your love; he wanted your life so that he could live. Our father was evil incarnate. You remember our birth?"

Remember my birth.

The words echoed through my head. Around the room, heads lowered in what looked like guilt, shame, and fear.

"And now, they're both gone." Hera backed away from her sister. "Mother loved him enough to lie down next to him in his sleep."

"She sacrificed herself so we could live," Demeter insisted.

"She could've stayed with us. But she loved him too much to be parted from him." Hera's golden eyes sparkled with unshed tears. "I only wish I had someone who would do the same for me."

"Don't look at me," Zeus said.

The tears dried up and her pupils flashed. "You're an asshole. I promised to be true to you for the rest of our lives, but you can't see past your own prick."

Zeus cocked his head. "Well, my prick is exceptionally long."

Hera growled and lunged for him. But her siblings stepped between them. Demeter and Poseidon came to her. Hades grabbed hold of Zeus's forearm. Hestia shook her head amid the commotion.

Hera looked at her siblings as though they were traitorous. She took a few steps backward, then a few more. When she felt the glass balcony door at her back, she turned, opened it, then stepped outside and leaped.

I gasped and ran across the room. By the time I got to the balcony, the sky was empty. I couldn't see down to the ground. But no screams trailed up to my ears.

"Don't worry about her," Zeus said dismissively. "She's a god. A few dozen stories won't kill her. Unfortunately."

"How long have you been here, darling?" Demeter asked, coming up to me.

"You just let her leave?" I said.

"She's a fully formed goddess," Zeus said.

"She's a distraught female with superpowers who has the ability to steal a soul. I think we should keep an eye on her for a few days . . . or years. At the very least, I think she needs a hug."

The siblings looked around at one another. Zeus threw his hands around his middle like he would be sick at the very thought.

"Now Zuzu," Demeter said in an admonishing

tone. "Don't be like that. You two did come into this world together. Why don't you dig deep into that dark heart of yours and go after her?"

"In the wise words of every younger sibling to an older one," he said through gritted teeth, "you are not my mother."

As the two gods continued to argue like young children, something shook loose in my mind. I stared at Demeter. For the few days that I'd been in her presence, she'd been calm, cool, and collected. She'd stood out as the mature leader of her powerful siblings. But watching her bicker with her brother made me realize something about the woman in the dreams I'd been having.

The slamming of the front door brought me back to the present. When I looked up, only five of the Olympians remained along with me, Loren, Bet, and Baros. The thunderous slam, I had to assume, came from Zeus leaving.

"Don't worry about Hera and Zuzu," Demeter said. "They fight all the time. You know what they say about a thin line between love and hate. Darling, why are you looking at me like that?"

"It's not you who has been visiting my dreams," I said. "It's been your mother."

"My mother is—"

"Asleep," I finished for her. "You said so yourself. Because she's not worshipped. No one praises her name. But she's not dead. She's somewhere, and she's been calling out to me."

The room went deathly still. None of the gods tried to deny my assertion.

"Rhea," I said, and just the mention of her name caused a swell of energy to rise around me. "She foresaw that your father would consume you. She was able to save Zeus. In turn, he saved all of you. She sees something else coming now, and she's been trying to tell me."

Hestia stepped forward. "Our mother came to you in a dream?"

I nodded at her hushed tone. Her blue eyes were clouded as though a surprise storm raced across the horizon. There was sorrow in the set of her high cheekbones.

"What did she say?" Hestia asked.

"She keeps telling me to wake up. In one dream, we were in the Parthenon. I saw many humans being sacrificed. That's what made me go back the other night, and then I found Socrates. This morning, she told me to remember your birth. What happened at your birth?"

Demeter turned from me and faced her siblings.

The healthy glow that always shone on her face went pale. A tremor ran through her voice as she spoke. "You don't think she would?"

None of her siblings answered her. They stared with shock shining out of their bright gazes.

Poseidon was the first to break the silence. His voice sounded ragged, like it had been bashed against the keel of a ship. "We need to go after her."

"Your mother?" I asked.

Four pairs of glowing eyes found mine.

"No," Poseidon said. "Hera."

I set my mouth to ask why, but I choked on the word. If the four individuals who knew the answer were immobilized with fear, and they were ancient gods, then I doubted I truly wanted to know the answer. Poseidon opened his mouth to answer my unasked question. I had the urge to duck lest I be pulled into a tidal wave of badness. But his sister cut him off before he could give it any voice.

"She wouldn't do that," Demeter insisted.

"You just heard her say it, Demi," Hestia said. "She said she wished Zeus had left her in Father's belly."

Demeter shook her head, the only Olympian still in doubt over whatever Hera's plan was. "But she can't do anything. No one worships him any longer.

And even if they did, she'd have to get them to Eleusis. We have time to find her and talk some sense into her."

"Actually . . ."

Everyone's head whipped to Loren.

"There's a party going on in Eleusis right now," she said.

"There's a tour company that promised people access to the Eleusinian Mysteries," I added.

"They do that every year," Demeter said. "Just a few dozen people dancing about and singing my name, not my father's."

"Well, this year the party went viral," Loren countered. She held up her phone to show first the invitation with the wheat wreath surrounding the peacock plume that symbolized Hera, and then a live feed of the college kids drinking, dancing, and reveling amidst the ruins of Eleusis. There had to be at least a hundred people in the crowd.

"That would be enough." Hestia's voice was faint.

"Enough to what?" I asked.

Demeter turned to me. The light in her eyes had gone out. "Enough to raise a god."

CHAPTER TWENTY-THREE

e sped down the streets of Athens with Baros at the wheel. With gods who could command earth, water, and fire, it was a wonder that none of them could fly to get us to Eleusis faster.

We were packed into the limo. Demeter and Bet sat to one side with me. Hestia, Poseidon, and Hades sat facing us. Loren rode in the front with Baros. Zeus had been MIA since storming out of Demeter's apartment after the argument with Hera.

There were many blocks along the road as it was a Friday night and parties were in full sway. Tourists filled the streets while citizens ducked off the beaten path and police put up blockades to keep the peace. None of the Grecians realized the danger presented to them by ancient deities who were in their midst. Nobody realized one of those deities was nearby and about to steal the souls of hundreds of people just like them.

We passed the Parthenon. Its columns looked luminous on the dark horizon. I saw the workers descending the steps, their work done for the day, disappearing into the night. It looked as though they were descending into the underworld. My mind fled back to Egypt and the workers falling into the chasm of a tomb.

"What did you mean when you said *raise a god*?" I turned to Demeter. "I thought you needed to feed off the worship and praise of willing souls to live?"

"We do," Demeter said. "Now that we're here."

"What about when you were born?" I asked, remembering her mother's ominous warning. "How exactly *were* you born?"

"I'm glad you don't remember." Demeter turned away from me and into Bet's shoulder. In an uncharacteristic show of humanity, Bet caressed her temple with his fingertips. "I wish I could forget, too."

It wasn't the first time she'd said those words to me. It wasn't the first time I'd asked how she was born. But now, I was starting to remember the first time this conversation had happened. I'd seen the evidence of the birth of a god firsthand.

Memories started coming back so fast my head was spinning. It started with what I'd seen in the dream of the ancient temples being built, and the workers dying. That hadn't been a dream; it was a memory.

I remembered the sweat pouring off shoulders in the hot sun. Bodies keeling over under the strain of the stone and marble. I recalled blood seeping out of barren eyes and soaking into the fields of wheat as two golden-haired gods emerged from the ether of existence. As Zeus and Hera opened their eyes for the first time of their existence, the human bodies dropped to the ground.

"We didn't ask to be born." Demeter's golden eyes were dim as they regarded me.

"Wheat is a symbol of sacrifice," I said. "The Ninnion Tablet—it doesn't depict how you *give* immortality to humans. It depicts your birth."

The Olympians either looked down at their hands or out the window. Not one would meet my gaze.

"On the tablet," I continued as the memories and the depictions on the tablet collided, "the wheat all around your heads and feet is a representation of the people who died. Hundreds were sacrificed to bring you into the world."

"No," Poseidon stated grimly. His square jaw was steely, but his clear eyes darkened. "Not hundreds of people. *Thousands* of human lives were taken to make way for us. Hades and Demeter were forged in the city of Atlantis. Hestia and I were brought forth in Memphis, Egypt. And Hera and Zeus came to life in Pompeii."

Atlantis, Memphis, Pompeii? "All those cities had civilizations that vanished," I said.

Bet looked over at me as though to say *I told you so.* But when a tremor wracked Demeter's shoulders, he turned and laced his long fingers with her shaking hands.

"Our father took human souls to give us life," Poseidon said. "We are made of stolen souls."

"But that's not how we live our lives," Demeter insisted. "We only take the willing, I told you. And we don't take their lives; we don't need to. They share their souls with us. It sustains us longer and allows us to give them long life. We are not parasites."

"But Hera's going to try to raise your parents with unwilling souls," I said. "Why?"

"I don't know." Demeter shook her head. "I don't know what she's thinking."

"Your mother was calling out to me from the grave . . . or wherever a goddess goes when they are no longer worshipped. She knew this was happening. She knew what Hera planned to do."

"Our mother still maintains a connection to each of us," Hestia answered. "She sacrificed herself so we could continue living."

"I thought Zeus saved you all from your father?"

"Our father had no care for humans," Hades said. "He looked at them as food."

"Perhaps that's why he fell out of favor." I said the words lightly, but grave faces stared back at me. I kept forgetting this was a sore spot with these people.

"He felt himself fading," Demeter said, "because the humans no longer called upon his name. And so, he turned to his children. *We* still called upon his name. So he tried to steal our very essence back. Zuzu was the last of his children he tried to consume. Zuzu was able to evade our father's treachery because of our mother's insight and rescue us."

"Zeus was able to get your father to release your souls?"

Demeter shook her head. "I told you, we don't have souls. Cronus pulled the humans' souls he'd sacrificed to create us straight from our bodies, leaving us as empty shells. Without the energy, we simply ceased to exist. Our bodies fell where we stood. We would have become mounds in the earth like our parents are now. Our minds were in the darkness. We were together, but so far apart. It was terrifying."

"How did Zeus free you?"

"The same way you would kill a demon. Zeus stabbed our father in the eyes with a lightning bolt. We were reborn—truly reborn. We never made another demon after that. Everyone comes to us of their own free will. It's a choice."

I believed her. "What about your mother?"

"She shared some of what was left of herself with our father. But it wasn't enough for their existence to last very long. It soothed him, though, and they both came to rest in Eleusis."

"She stayed with him after what he'd done to her children?" I asked.

Demeter shrugged. "She still loved him. Who understands what the heart wants?" Her gaze slid to Bet's. Then, realizing they had an audience, the two of them jerked away as though they'd been caught with their hands in the cookie jar.

"Anyway," Demeter continued, "you were

horrified when you learned how we came to be. I suppose that's when you made the Ninnion Tablet. Then you forgot us. And here we are again."

"The dirt doesn't lie," I said, reciting the one constant truth in my life. No matter what people tried to hide, it would one day be dug up and revealed to all. "Did you take the tablet from the museum?"

"I did," Demeter admitted. "I didn't like having my greatest shame on display for all to see, even if most people didn't know what it meant."

I tilted my head back against the headrest and closed my eyes. More people keeping secrets from me. And because of it, more humans were about to die.

We pulled up to Eleusis and the temple, then filed out of the car. There was a crowd of humans out amidst the ruins. There were far more than a hundred people—closer to two hundred, maybe even three—spread out among the grassy knolls and fallen stones. The party was in full swing. People were dressed in their clubbing finest, as well as in old Greek garb to resemble the gods. Girls sashayed their bodies in peplos. Guys wearing togas made lewd gestures. There were even a few bare-chested men with shields and swords trying to emulate the Spartans.

Standing atop the highest pillar on the mound at the center of the ruins was Hera. As though she sensed her siblings, she turned to us. Even from this distance, I saw her glowing eyes narrow.

"Hera," Demeter shouted. Music blared, people yelled, but I got the sense that Hera heard her sister loud and clear. "Hera, stop this now."

Hera turned away from Demeter with a haughty defiance. She raised her arms up into the night's sky. A ripple went through the crowd. The spines of every person dancing and drinking straightened. As one, they turned to face Hera. Their eyes glowed brightly, just like the initiates during the rites a few nights ago before their souls were offered up to the gods.

It wasn't a joyous hum that sang through the crowd. This energy rubbed my skin the wrong way. It left behind a foul taste in my mouth. It burned my eyes. When the sickening hum died down, hundreds of blackened, red-rimmed eyes turned on us.

"Shit," said one of the Olympians. I wasn't sure which one. It may have been all of them.

CHAPTER TWENTY-FOUR

Four gods, two Immortals, a Spartan warrior, and a human woman walked into a temple. It sounded like the beginning of a bad joke. But I stood in the reality of it. The eight of us faced off against one neglected deity and a horde of mindless humans who were now under her control. This was not how I'd planned to spend this evening.

"We have to get to her," Demeter said. "We can still reason with her."

"Demi, she's stolen hundreds of souls." Hestia looked aghast. "She's past reasoning."

"Nia," Loren called beside me.

"Loren, hold on." I kept my attention on the gods and goddesses before me.

"We can't kill her," Demi cried.

"It looks like she's about to try to kill us," Hades stated.

"But she can't kill us," Demeter said. "We're family."

"I seem to remember you saying the same thing just before Father dearest swallowed you whole," Poseidon pointed out.

"Nia," Loren said again. Her voice sounded panicked. I'd never heard Loren sound that way. I turned to her. Panic rose in my own chest when I saw why.

Her eyes were slowly turning black, the blue receding and red bleeding around the edges. It was obvious by her expression that she was fighting the possession. Baros stood beside her. His jaw clenched, his dark eyes wide, his handsome face stony as he looked between Loren and the goddess on the hilltop who was taking his lover's soul away.

"I can't stop it." Loren gasped, and then took in a series of shallow breaths. "I can feel her in my head."

Loren ran her hands through her hair. Then she pulled at the roots as though she could yank Hera's grip on her spirit away. It was a losing battle as her blue irises were nearly swallowed whole.

Demeter stepped between us. "You need to give me your soul."

"No." Loren jerked away from Demeter and reached for me. I took her hands in my own, but I couldn't hold onto her life force. It was beyond my grasp.

"It's the only way to keep her safe," Demeter insisted, speaking to me instead of Loren, as though I were her keeper. "But she has to give it to me freely. And she has to do it quickly before Hera has her completely in hand. I'm surprised she's lasted this long without succumbing."

I looked at Loren's struggling face. A red ring burned brighter and brighter at the edges of her eyes. I thought of Socrates, dirty and discarded in a corner as he begged for death. I couldn't let that happen to Loren.

"Do you promise you'll give it back?" I said to Demeter.

"Yes, of course."

"Loren . . .?" I had to ask. I couldn't force her. She had to make this decision.

Sweat dotted Loren's brow as she struggled with the lesser of two evils. "Fine," she hissed through clenched teeth.

Demeter held out her hand. "You have to give it freely, pet."

Even through the dark redness, Loren glared. "I

give you my soul ... freely ... for now."

"Good enough." Demeter's eyes turned golden, and I watched as Loren's soul was sucked from her body. Because it was no longer a struggle, the energy flowed freely and quickly from woman to goddess.

It was just in time. With the humans under her control, Hera whipped her head to her siblings. A wicked glint lit her fiery eyes. She raised her hands. As one, the humans did the same. Only most of their hands weren't empty. They held beer bottles. A shower of bottles blocked out the moon and prepared to rain down on us.

Before any glass could hit, boulders rose from the ground. The rocks formed a protective shield above our heads, and shards of glass rained down around us. When the storm finished, Hestia stepped to the front.

"I can't believe she just did that." Hestia's face filled with anger.

She took a menacing step toward her sister. Humans ran into her path. She shoved them aside like they were gnats flitting over her picnic.

I caught up to her, grabbing her shoulder. "Wait, we can't hurt these people. They're innocents."

The innocents continued charging us from all sides, surrounding us, pummeling us with their fists and costume weapons. I left my blade strapped to my thigh. I could incapacitate those who came at me with some well-placed punches and kicks that would maim but not murder.

The ground began to rumble beneath our feet. I looked over and saw Hades raising his hands. Stones rose, blocking the path of the advancing humans.

From behind, Poseidon called forth water from some underground well. The splash knocked down a few dozen people, but others kept coming from all sides.

"We need to stick together," Baros said, taking command like the soldier he was.

"No," Bet said. "We need to spread apart and take them in quadrants."

The two men faced off, metaphorically measuring the size of their balls as the humans advanced. Now wasn't the time to air out ancient grievances. They were on the same side in this battle. Both Demeter and I stepped to them, likely prepared to deliver the same zip-up-your-pants-and-put-it-away pep talk, but Hestia beat us to it.

"We don't have time for this," she shouted. "The wise thing is to take down the root of this problem—Hera. We'll cut a path through the humans directly to her. We'll strike on three."

"Wait, do you mean *on* three?" Loren asked. "Or do you mean three and *then* we go?"

Hestia took a split second to glare at her before taking command again. "On three, ready?"

She counted off. We charged forward on three. Bodies fell around us as we plowed through. It felt like a bad action movie. But it was working. The humans were no match for our immortal strength and a badass swordswoman. In fact, it was said badass swordswoman and her Chosen lover who made their way to Hera ahead of the rest of us.

With Hera busy maneuvering hundreds of minds to do her bidding, she was caught off guard when Loren lifted her sword to the goddess's glowing eyes. All human activity stopped as Hera focused on the blade hovering at the tip of her nose. I felt a moment of pride swell through my chest . . . until a sword was aimed at Loren's throat.

"Drop it, Lolo."

Loren turned wide eyes on Baros. "I never thought I'd say this, but, Lenny, you need to point that thing somewhere else."

"Sorry, it's not about you." Baros smiled sadly, but he didn't lower his weapon. His hot glare turned on Bet. "It's about him."

With the humans no longer swarming around

us, we formed a semi-circle at the crumbling steps of the temple below where Hera, Baros, and Loren stood. Energy still hummed in the night. The air was thick with the struggle of minds trying to break free of a power greater than the alcohol and drugs they'd consumed.

"I pledged my life, my sword, to you gods," Baros said, eying each of the Olympians standing at the bottom of the stairs. "With all your power, you let him and his savages ravage my homeland for centuries."

"Baros, we keep out of the affairs of humans," Demeter said. "You know that."

"No. You choose your battles, just as you choose your initiates and your bedmates. I have free will. And now I'm making a choice of my own. If you won't fight the continued assault against my homeland, then I'll bring back someone who can."

In the standoff, a sheet of copy paper fluttered by my feet. It was an invitation to tonight's event. The lettering was written in black and white. A wreath of wheat crowned the letterhead surrounding a plume of peacock feathers. Peacock feathers—the symbol of the goddess of fertility.

It was all making sense now. Back in Budapest, the blogger who was denied entry, the stack of invitations in the church office, the browser displaying the invite in an online forum. Baros had sent out the invitations for hundreds to come here to a ritual led by Hera.

"Cronus would have never allowed an invasion onto the lands he occupied," Baros said.

"Baros . . ." Demeter's voice was firm. "Put the sword down and stop this nonsense. This isn't about you. It's about Hera."

"Wrong again, sister." Hera sounded smug. "It's never been about me. But now it will be. I'm calling Daddy."

"Damn, girl." Loren shook her head. "You've got brother *and* daddy issues."

I closed my eyes and turned to Demeter. "Can you shut her up, please?" I chucked my thumb at Loren, whose sword still held steady at Hera's nose. "Before she gets herself killed."

"Your pet still has her will," Demeter answered. "Just like you do, Baros. You don't know what it was like when my father was alive. He swallowed whole civilizations to get what he wanted. He'll do the same to Greece, starting with these people here in Eleusis."

"So long as he aims his eyes at Turkey," Baros said, "we'll get along just fine."

Hera's eyes turned away from Loren and flashed at Baros. "Kill her."

Baros sighed. His broad chest rose and fell with reluctance. "Put it down, Lolo."

"Look at that." Loren's voice was sarcastic. "You're giving me a choice, and I'm choosing to stab the bitch's eyes out."

Baros sighed again. Then things went in slow motion. I saw his wrist flick. Loren's eyes flinched as she took in his movement. The blade of Baros's sword glinted in the moonlight as it swiped toward her. But the space where it swiped was empty.

Loren ducked and rolled out of reach. She tumbled down the hill and landed at my feet, popping up before I could reach down for her. Her dark eyes flashed murder.

"He was really going to do it," Loren fumed. "Oh, that fridge between us is not only on the ground, it's in a freakin' trash compactor."

With Hera's gaze free once more, the humans were back in play. But instead of attacking us, their voices rose in a chant, calling out an ancient name. The ground began shaking again, and we all toppled. I turned to Hades, but he shook his head.

"That's not me," Hades said. His fists were

clenched at his sides, not using the dominion he had over the earth.

"Oh, God." Hestia's face dripped with worry. "Our father. He's waking."

The humans' voices rose louder and louder as they sang out Cronus's name. If the energy of the stolen souls felt heavy in the night's air, the energy calling forth the slumbering Titan felt like it would suffocate me with each breath.

"If our father wakes," Demeter warned, "it could be hell on earth. He'll tear their souls right off their bones to stay alive. We have to stop this now. I'm sorry, Nia, but we need to sacrifice these few hundred human lives to stop the rise of a monster who will feast on the entirety of humanity. We have to kill them before Cronus can rise."

Now coupled with the sensation of suffocating, my stomach roiled and bile rose in my throat at the thought of what had to be done. Because Demeter was right. If we couldn't get Hera to give these people their will back, then we'd have to silence them to keep Cronus in his forced respite. But these innocents wouldn't be the only ones forfeiting their lives.

"If we have to kill these humans, then you'll have to take out your sister," I said.

She shut her eyes briefly. I could feel her gulp down the lump in her throat. "I know," she whispered.

Demeter looked as despondent as I felt. But we had no other choice.

We all sprang into action. We tunneled through the humans, gunning up the steps to the temple and the goddess of fertility who was trying to birth a monster. Bet made it there before either of us.

Baros's grin was feral as he raised his sword to hack into his oldest enemy. Baros may have been a Spartan fighter, but Bet was an ancient warrior. Bet evaded the sword by stepping into Baros. With an elbow to Baros's solar plexus, Bet freed the sword from Baros's hand. Instead of either man picking up the weapon, they went at it hand to hand. But the ground they stood upon shook. They lost their footing and fell apart. Baros rolled down the hill. Bet nearly fell into a crevice that opened in the ground.

Demeter reached the top of the hill before I did and faced her sister. Hera lunged for Demeter, knocking the golden-haired deity to the ground. Demeter sprang up, putting her hands around Hera's throat.

The ground was still shaking as though Cronus was tossing restlessly in his bed. I stood over the two women. After pulling my blade from its holster, I handed it hilt-first to Demeter. She didn't look directly at me, as her hands were still occupied around her sister's throat. But I knew she saw the blade in her peripheral vision.

"Hera, please," Demeter begged. "Stop this."

But Hera didn't. She struggled beneath her sister, kicking and screeching like a banshee. Demeter grabbed for the dagger. She held it over Hera's eyes.

Hera stopped struggling. A manic glint lit her glowing eyes. "Do it," she challenged.

Demeter's hand trembled under the slight weight of the blade. Her eyes watered as she gazed down at her sister. She took a deep, ragged breath and raised the dagger. Her brothers and sister came and stood at her back. None of them stepped in to stop her.

Beneath us, the ground cracked open. The columns around the temples shook, forming a backbone as a god wrestled himself from the underworld. The blade fell from Demeter's hand as she stared, transfixed.

Two blank eyes pulled up from the ground and glared at her. A hand reached up from a boulder, flexing its fingers. The hand rose.

Hera rolled out from under Demeter's hold.

"Father, it's me," she called, sounding every bit the toddler who stood on the doorstep waiting for her dad to come home from work.

I grabbed for Demeter and pulled her away. It was just in time. The hand reached out and closed around Hera. It brought her into the air. From below the blank eyes, a mouth of black hollowness opened.

"Father?" Hera's voice wobbled. "Father, no."

But Cronus did not heed his child's plea. Hera's body dropped closer and closer until it was just inside the black hole that was the father she'd missed so desperately. Before Hera could be consumed, a lightning bolt struck the right eye of the Titan.

Zeus swooped in, another lightning bolt in one hand. The other hand he wrapped around Hera's waist and pulled. "Let the people go, Hera."

He flung the second bolt at his father's left eye. The head of the Titan reared back. He crashed to the ground, knocking us off our feet. Still, Cronus did not release his daughter from his hungry grip.

"Hera, let them go," Zeus shouted as he pulled her to him. "It's the only way he'll release you."

"I'd rather go with him than stay here with the lot of you," was Hera's reply. She shoved against

Zeus's chest, but he didn't release her. Neither did Cronus.

The large hand pulled downward, bringing Hera and Zeus closer to his mouth, which opened wider. I felt the wind kick up, but it had nothing to do with air pressure. It was Cronus sucking the life out of the two youngest Olympians.

Zeus let Hera go. Without him tethering her to this world, she descended faster into Cronus's mouth. Hera shrieked and covered her eyes as her father began sucking out the souls she'd stolen. And then she shrieked again as she fell and impacted the ground.

Zeus stood over her, a lightning sword in his grip. His father's disembodied hand was at his feet. But Cronus was not done.

He'd gotten a taste of life and looked eager for more. Another hand reached up from the earth. But this hand did not belong to Cronus.

Rhea's head poked out of the earth. Rich soil and flowers caked her wheat-colored hair. There was still light in her golden eyes. With a surprisingly strong grip, she reached for her husband and wrapped her hand around his chin. She opened her mouth, as though she were going to kiss her lover. But instead, she sucked the lives out of him.

When the life had left Cronus's eyes, she pulled his body down into the mound where they rested. It looked as though she were taking the green grass as a comforter and covering them up for the night. Before she laid her head down, she looked out at her children.

Her gaze rested on each in turn. No words passed between Rhea and her offspring, just lingering gazes, soft, sad smiles, and quiet tears. Her gaze came to Hera last, and Rhea lifted an eyebrow.

I didn't have a mother, but I still knew that look. It clearly stated, *You're in big trouble, missy.*

Hera was still on the ground. She'd propped herself on her elbows, but her eyes were downcast. She chewed at her lower lip and nodded. Then she lifted her head and opened her eyes wide.

A surge of energy went out into the night as hundreds of souls were returned to their original owners. The humans collapsed onto the ground with the force. The silence that followed was eerie as hundreds of human bodies littered the ground like bugs after a fumigation.

Rhea gave an approving nod and prepared to sink back into the earth. As she did, she found my gaze. A small smile tilted her lips as she acknowledged me. I could do nothing but stare as the ground closed over her and her husband.

Though Rhea clearly had enough energy to walk the earth, she chose to stay in slumber with her murderous, infanticidal, possibly psychotic husband. And Loren called Zane and my relationship codependent. *Pfft.*

Demeter was the first to move. She rose and took a few steps toward her fallen sister, who was still crumpled on the ground.

"Don't you touch her," Zeus demanded, coming to stand protectively over Hera. "You would've killed her."

"Zuzu," Demeter began, "what she did—"

"Don't come any closer," he ground out, another bolt flashing into his hand.

The ground still rumbled beneath our feet, but it was tiny tremors. The human bodies that littered the ground shuddered. I didn't have my full faculties, but I knew something like this could never happen again. We couldn't just let Hera run wild on an earth filled with billions of souls she could one day wake up and decide to give to the father she missed. I started to take the few steps to come to Demeter's side.

"You have a beautiful body, Tisa," Zeus said.

"One I'm sad I have yet to partake of. But I will rip it to shreds if you lay a hand on my wife."

The venom in his sweet words called me up short. I stopped my advance and stood next to Demeter, who also stood impotent. Neither of us dared to cross the line toward them.

Zeus bent down to lift Hera into his arms.

"Let me go," Hera screeched. She wrenched her body away from him. "Don't touch me. I hate you."

"I know." Zeus locked his arms around her. "I've got you."

"Let me go," she sobbed, but the fight had gone out of her.

"No," he whispered. "I can't."

"I hate you," Hera whispered.

"I can't stand you either." He rubbed the hair away from her face and placed a kiss there.

"Wow," Loren whispered from behind my shoulder. "It's like a live version of *Jerry Springer*."

I had nothing to say. I watched as the acrid venom that had persisted between the two allowed for something deeper to rise. After a while, Hera stopped fighting and rested her head on Zeus's chest, in the space just below his chin and between his pecs where I imagined his heart beat.

CHAPTER TWENTY-FIVE

No one died that night. The revelers were bruised and beat up. A few of the injuries were major but none life-threatening. People awoke hours later, exclaiming it had been the best party of their lives and wanting to do it again sooner rather than later.

I sat on the terrace of the Olympian Hotel, staring at the Parthenon. Poseidon came up and sat beside me. His long brown legs stretched out before him, and his dark locks lay limp on his shoulders. He looked exhausted, like he'd just washed up on the shore.

"Did you find him?" I asked.

By him, I meant Baros. He'd disappeared in the

melee after he'd rolled down the hill when the Titans woke up. He'd left not a trace behind.

"No," Poseidon replied. "But I'm sure your brother will have an eye out for him now that Leonidas is no longer under our protection."

I was so exhausted I didn't bother telling him Bet and I weren't related. I wondered if Bet would stick his neck out for me the way these six did for one another. And that included Zeus literally putting his life on the line to save Hera after the senseless destruction she'd caused.

"Can't Zeus do anything about it?" I asked. "Since he holds Baros's soul?"

"My brother is preoccupied at this time."

Zeus had disappeared with Hera, despite my objections that she was a danger to humanity.

"Like your family isn't screwed up," the golden god had thrown at me before spiriting away with a subdued Hera. They, too, had not left a trace as to their whereabouts, and no one seemed concerned that an immature Lothario and a petulant sociopath were out unsupervised.

Demeter entered with Loren at her side. "Here's your girl," Demeter said. "I trimmed the edges around her personality a bit to make her more obedient."

Loren glowered at the goddess. When she did, it was with her blue eyes and not the dark, fathomless depths she'd had to sport last night.

Demeter ignored Loren's glare and focused on me. "Now that she's housebroken, you two could stay a while."

I reached out and grabbed Loren's forearm. Though Demeter was a goddess, Loren was a force to be reckoned with. I had no desire to be in the middle of another knock-down, drag-out battle.

I shook my head as I leaned into Loren. She crossed her arms and kept her glower, but she also took on some of my weight.

"Loren and I are going sailing. She's lost a yacht; I mean, a lover. So I figured I'd get her on top of another one. It's what besties do when a douchebag stomps on one of their hearts."

"I thought I was your bestie?" Demeter sounded sulky. Her full cheeks turned sullen and her bright eyes dimmed.

The despondent look tugged at my heartstrings, but I stood my ground. "If we're going to remain friends, which I think I'd like, you can't keep secrets from me anymore."

She opened her mouth to protest, but I held up my hand.

"Regardless of whether I forget what happened," I said. "If you'd been honest with me when I first got here, I may have been able to help sooner."

Demeter pursed her lips, but then she nodded. "I screwed up. By not telling you, but also by neglecting my own sister. I think it's clear we're all paying attention now. Nia, please trust me when I say that we will take care of this."

"I believe you, Demi."

"So maybe you won't be such a stranger for the next millennium?"

I smiled. "I'll be around. Especially now that I know where to get devotional discounts on designer dresses."

I embraced her. She wrapped her arms around me tightly. We held on for what felt like an eternity until finally we released each other. That part felt too familiar—the letting go of a friend after we'd faced tragedy.

"Keep an eye on that one," she whispered in my ear.

"Who? Loren? Her bark is worse than her bite. Mostly."

"She has a bite to her, all right. Unlike any other soul I've held before."

I glanced between my new BFF and my old one. I wasn't sure if there was a hint of jealousy in Demeter's gaze, or if that was true caution.

Before I headed out, I embraced the other Olympian gods as well. Poseidon wrapped me up in his big arms, the scent of the ocean wafting from his locks. Hades slipped another gem into my hand before letting me go. Even Hestia came in for an awkward pat on the back.

"Don't be a stranger," she said. "I'm a decent sister, but I'm not so good in the whole friend department."

I nodded my agreement. Then I headed to the elevator with Loren. Our bags were packed and in the lobby. With no adventure left, it was time to depart Greece.

"Are you sure you don't want immortality?" I asked Loren as we descended.

"If I did want to live forever, it would have to be for myself. I couldn't be beholden to another entity like that. I think that bitch moved my organs around."

I chuckled. The doors of the elevator opened, spilling us into the lobby. "I'm sorry about Baros."

Loren shrugged. "It was too good to be true. My

own Spartan in shining armor. I'm not meant for that."

"Every girl deserves to be swept off her feet occasionally."

"I like to stand on my own, thank you very much. Men make you wobbly."

"Wanna stop in the restaurant for some ice cream?" I said. "To help with the breakup."

"Who needs ice cream when we could go have another adventure? What do you say, wanna swing by Egypt and raid a pharaoh's tomb? Or sail to Scotland and fish for the Loch Ness monster?"

I chuckled. I just wanted some quiet time on a boat. No adventure. No artifacts. And definitely no mythical creatures.

"Nessie is gonna have to wait." Loren smirked. "It looks like a knight is sweeping into our girl time. Sexy beast incoming."

I felt the tickle at my throat then. I hadn't been paying too much attention because Bet was still upstairs with Demeter. When I turned and looked in the direction Loren faced, I saw Tres.

"I'm going to grab a drink at the bar," Loren said.

She dashed away before I could latch onto her. It took everything I had to hold still while Tres made his way to me. I hadn't called or texted him since I'd gotten back from my little excursion to Rome. I hadn't had time to think about what I'd say to him.

I took a deep breath and lifted my chin. Either my eyes were weary from the less-than-restful sleep I'd had last night, or Tresor Mohandis had gotten even dreamier since the last time I'd seen him. He was dressed in a dark blue shirt that set off his honey-brown coloring. His jacket was off, slung over his left shoulder. The dress shirt was rolled up past his elbows, showing off his defined forearms and hinting at the corded biceps beneath. He wore a grin on his face that didn't look annoyed or put out with me in the slightest for not getting back to him. It had only been two days, after all. We'd been apart for hundreds of years.

"You look awful," he said when he reached me.

I felt my face tighten with annoyance, balling my fists instead of running my fingers through my hair like I self-consciously wanted to. But then, Tres pulled me into him and ran his fingers through my hair himself. Though he'd insulted me, his eyes took me in like he wanted to muss me up even more.

"Did I miss the adventure?" he asked with a grin. His fingers came to rest just above my ear.

"You did. It was one for the storybooks."

"Can I offer you another one?" Those dark eyes gleamed with invitation.

"What kind of adventure?" My lips stayed parted after I spoke. They had to. My nostrils were too busy flaring to take in oxygen.

"Me, on a boat, in the middle of the ocean, with lots of wine." He leaned down, cupping his hand around my ear and whispering as though he didn't want to be overheard. "And an old treasure map. But we both know where that will lead."

I grinned as he pulled away, resting my hand on his chest to feel his strong, steady heartbeat. The rhythm was a familiar tune. I wanted to lay my head there and relearn its song. But . . .

"Can I take a rain check?" I asked. "Recently, a friend reminded me that the unexamined life isn't worth living."

I thought of Socrates and the twinkle that had been in his opaque eyes when he'd said those words to me at his farewell party. I hoped his soul was at ease.

"I've been examining other people's lives for hundreds of years," I continued. "I think it's time I do a little soul-searching of my own."

Tres didn't protest. Neither did he let me go. His

thumb trailed over my lower lip. I felt my mouth water, that hunger coming back to my gut.

"You should know that I always collect on my debts," he said.

"You should remember I always pay my bills," I countered.

He grinned again. His lips were parted when he leaned in and brushed his mouth against mine, but he didn't press his advantage like he'd done in the past. It was me who sank my teeth into his upper lip and then my tongue into his mouth.

I had control for all of five seconds before he wrenched my head to the side and claimed my mouth. His tongue was demanding as it reached into my crevices, his lips hot as they tugged at my need. He left me too quickly with an unquenched longing, an aching yearning, and shallow, dizzying breaths.

When he pulled away, he said, "I'm going to see you sooner rather than later, Dr. Rivers."

My voice was low and husky when I made my comeback. "I wouldn't be surprised, Mr. Mohandis."

I watched him walk away. Just as I had to steel myself to stay put when I saw him coming my way, I had to hold myself still as the distance increased between us.

Damn. What was it about that man that made

me act so out of character? I'd be finding out soon, it seemed. But for now, I wanted to get back to girl time. I turned to find Loren, but I was met with an unexpected sight.

"Hi," I managed to get out.

"*Bonjour*," Zane said.

CHAPTER TWENTY-SIX

I looked back over my shoulder to the space where Tres had left out the door, then back to where Zane stood, immobile. His eyes were also fixed on the door where Tres had exited.

Zane's full lips were slightly parted. His eyebrows were squished together. The skin between his forehead crinkled. His normally hooded gaze was open and wide. His eyes blinked rapidly, as though trying to make sense of puzzle pieces scattered before him.

I swallowed and then reacted like someone who'd been caught doing something she shouldn't have. I reached for the redirect. "What are you doing here?"

Slowly, painfully slowly, Zane's gaze found mine. He searched my face as though seeing me for the first time. He blinked a few times as though trying to bring me into focus before he answered. The words came slowly, like English was his second language. It wasn't. But the French accent was thick on his tongue.

"I decided to take a chance and chase after you," he said. "But it would appear you have already been caught."

"No..." I looked again to the door Tres had left through. "He was just...I didn't...We were..."

Zane waited patiently, but it was in vain. I had no idea how to finish that sentence. I didn't owe him an explanation. I could do what I wanted with whom I wanted. Just the other night, he'd had another woman in his arms. We were broken up.

"I'm trying to find myself," I said finally. Lamely.

Zane cocked his head. His brows straightened as he regarded me. He swept his eyes over the length of me, like an inattentive husband might do when his wife asked if he noticed anything different about her. But that would never work with Zane. He knew every detail, down to noticing when I switched up the shade of my eyeliner. Nothing had changed since the last time he'd seen me.

I tried again. "Everyone has memories of me that I don't have. Sometimes, I don't know who I am. You want me to be one way—"

"No," he said quietly. "I have never asked you to be anything but who you are."

I crossed my arms over my chest, balling my hands into fists under my armpits. "Well, I don't know who that is right now."

"And so you kiss Tresor to find yourself?" he asked.

I jerked my arms to my sides. My posture went rigid as I glared at him.

"And you come to Rome and sleep with me—to what, lose yourself?"

Heat rose to my cheeks. An angry outburst bubbled up my throat. But the look on his face was like a bucket of icy water thrown atop my head. My head dipped. I stared at the ground, my gaze going hazy with mounting tears.

"I'm not trying to hurt you, Zane."

"And yet, you are."

His voice was so soft, so quiet. Part of me wanted him to yell, to rage. But he didn't. I glanced over to see that his hands were also balled, but in a loose fist, as though he wasn't sure if he wanted to hold on or let go.

"You hurt me every time. And I still keep coming back for more." His grip slackened. He straightened his fingers, flexing them as far as they would go.

I felt the world rocking around me. How had things gotten so out of control? I needed something to hold onto. I stepped up to him, but he held out his hand. Not open in welcome. His palm faced up in the universal motion for *stop*. His fingers didn't touch me, but it felt like they'd shoved me backward.

"Don't," he said. He seemed to say it more to himself than to me. "You know, this is the definition of insanity. I wait hundreds of years for you, for just a few moments in time, and it always ends with you running away from me. Yet, I keep coming back, expecting it to be different each time."

His voice was softer than a whisper, but it rattled its way through my bones. It felt harder than when Cronus shook the ground the other night, louder than Hera's cries for attention. I felt it pulling me down into a dark mound deep in the earth. Whatever I was made of, be it energy or spirit, it felt like it was being sucked out of me with the quiet desolation of his voice.

"Zane?" I reached out my hand, but he took a step back.

"I need some space," he said.

I pulled my hand away, but the movement felt like I was lifting a heavy boulder with the effort.

"Okay," I said, but the two syllables were heavy on my tongue.

Zane's gaze found mine. His dark eyes were clouded with hurt and confusion. I couldn't stand to see his pain. I took another step toward him, but he retreated and I stumbled.

We stood there. Only a few feet separated us, but the chasm felt wider than the Mediterranean. There had never been empty space between us. I didn't know what to do with it.

"This is confusing," he said with a humorless laugh.

"I know. For me too."

He looked at me. For the first time in this lifetime, I couldn't read his gaze. "I need you to do something for me," he said.

I nodded my head in agreement before he asked.

"Don't call me," he said. "Don't text me. Don't email me. Don't try to find me. Just give me some space."

I felt my heart plummet to the floor. When I looked once more into his dark gaze, I almost wished there was a red rim there so he would do what I wanted and stop hurting. But there wasn't.

Zane blinked, and then he stepped away from me. Without a touch, without a kiss, without another word, he was gone. He left through the same door as Tres.

CHAPTER TWENTY-SEVEN

I stared out at the setting sun over the Mediterranean. Where the sky met the sea, it looked like a mashup of black and blue. Pretty much how I was feeling right now.

A pair of arms came around me. In one hand was a wine glass. I took it and downed it in two gulps.

"Does drinking and driving apply to boats?" Loren asked as she sat down next to me with a glass in her other hand.

I shrugged. I planned to get stupid-drunk and then dock somewhere in the middle of the ocean. Or maybe I should switch that order? We were taking a true girls' trip, away from boys and any other distractions, in order to mend our bruised and broken hearts. There were no cares about getting a groove back right now. Men were not welcome on the dance floor of this boat.

"Nia? Are you sure you want to take this trip right now? I wouldn't hold it against you if you wanted to go after Zane."

I shook my head. Zane was never coy or cryptic. He always said exactly what he meant. When he said he didn't want to see me, I knew I should believe him. Though it was still hard to comprehend that those words had come out of the mouth that used to worship me with words and kisses.

"You could take this trip with Tres instead," she offered.

"We could go and look for Baros," I challenged.

She held up her hands in a placating fashion. "Touché."

"Zane and Tres know what they want. I'm the one who's confused. I just need a moment to figure out my life away from both of them, away from all men."

"Then out in the middle of the ocean it is." Loren took a sip from her glass. Then she rose and headed for the back of the ship. "I'll go and pull up the anchor."

I lounged in the deck chair and put my feet up, staring out at the bruised sky. As the darkness of night settled more firmly, the color evened out. It looked like there had never been a tear on the horizon. All it had taken was the passage of time for things to settle. I had that in spades. I just didn't know what to do with it.

Once again I felt the weight of my age crashing around my shoulders. Growing old was easy. It was the growing up bit that was hard to do.

"Let me help you with that," said a deep voice with a bit of a burr.

I sat up straight, my senses on full alert. My bare feet slapped onto the deck floor as I leaned forward in my chair.

I couldn't see who spoke to Loren, but I recognized that Scottish accent. People from the United Kingdom visited Greece all the time, but that burr was older than modern times. I stood slowly, knowing exactly who I would see when I made my way to the back of the boat. When my eyes confirmed it, I groaned and made my way over to them.

"Loren, back away from him."

"But he's so cute," she said, twirling a lock of her blonde hair. "Can't we take him with us?"

All her memories and hurt that had been caused by a certain Spartan king appeared to flee her mind as she stared at the broad, ginger-haired man on the dock. He stood well over six feet with a strong upper body that looked as though it were made for jousting. When he smiled, twin dimples rose on each side of his chiseled jaw.

"Hello, Dr. Rivers," he said.

Loren's grin fell. "Damn, Nia. Do you have dibs on every cute guy on the freaking planet?"

"What do you want, Lance?" I demanded, ignoring Loren's pout.

Lance grinned. "Can't I just stop by to say hi to an old friend?"

"In that case, you should hurry up and go find them."

"Are you still mad about *Seure?*" Lance asked.

He was referring to an ancient sword used in a battle against the Saxons. "That sword belongs in a museum."

"No, lass, it belonged to my ancestors and is therefore my birthright. You were poaching on our lands."

Technically, he was right. About fifty years ago, I'd gotten word that a group of archaeologists had found interesting artifacts on a burial site believed to be the location of the great Battle of Edington that occurred in the eighth century. I may have flashed my credentials and dipped in to see if the fabled sword was there. It was. But Lance had beaten me to it.

"You know you need permission to come onto our lands," Lance admonished from his place on the dock, his youthful grin belying his true age.

"I was just doing my job," I said, feeling superior as I stood over him on the deck.

He smirked up at me, completely uncowed. "Archaeology is your hobby. The recovery and protection of magical artifacts is the very reason for my existence."

I tilted my chin and regarded him, trying to uncover his angle. "What does he want?"

Lance bit at his lip. But in the end, he held up his hands like he was ready to come clean. "He needs a favor."

"Then he should get someone who works for him to do the job. Not a little hobbyist like me." I reached for Loren and made to turn us both away.

"It has to do with the Grail," Lance shouted up to me.

That stopped me in my tracks. My spine straightened, and I slowly turned back to see Lance grinning. He knew he had me with that one word.

"What about it?" I asked, feigning a nonchalance that neither of us bought.

"I can't discuss it off hallowed ground. You'll have to come to the castle."

I rocked back on my heels. Then I nearly kicked up my feet to dance a jig. My voice was breathless when I spoke. "Arthur is inviting me to the castle?"

"Desperate times call for desperate measures, it would seem. So, can I tell the boss to expect you?" Lance asked.

The answer was yes. It was *hell yes*. But I schooled my features. I wasn't that easy. I cocked my hip and shoved my hand onto my waist to present some modicum of cool.

"Well, Lancelot," I said. "You go and tell The Arthur that I'll make some time to come and see him. After I handle some important business of my own."

Lancelot grinned. Then he bowed his ginger head like the courtly hero that he was. "I'm at your service, my lady." He spared a wink for Loren and then took off down the dock.

The moment he was out of sight, I dashed to the helm of the ship, preparing to take off across the seas. Loren was at my heels.

"What just happened?" she asked. "You called him Lancelot. You said Arthur."

"Yup."

"Like Lancelot and Arthur?"

"Hmm."

"Wait? There really is a King Arthur?"

"Not *the* Arthur, *The* Arthur."

"Yeah." Loren shook her head slowly. "I don't get the distinction."

"I'll explain on the way."

"Where are we going?"

"To Camelot."

The adventure continues as Nia and Loren
take a seat at the Round Table in
Templar Scrolls
Book Three of the Nia Rivers Adventures.

Grab your copy today!